LOOK
NO HANDS

by

COLLEEN

PEARSON

RAMPANT HORSE BOOKS

First published in Great Britain in 1997 by Rampant Horse,
The Wells House, Holywell Road, Malvern Wells,
Worcestershire WR14 4LH

British Library Cataloguing in Publication Data

A catalogue record for this book is available
from the British Library

ISBN 1 898839 62 X

Designed and produced by Images.
Printed and Bound in Great Britain.

ACKNOWLEDGEMENTS

I am indebted to the following: Paul Forrester O'Neill, creative writing tutor, Brenda Basnett, Hazel Cartwright, Les Hill and Jean Simcock of the Endon Writers' Group for their encouragement, advice and ideas. I wish them all success, they deserve it.

George Cooper and Terry James for being brave enough to read the first draft and to offer constructive advice.

Roger Butters for introducing me to the publishers.

All at Rampant Horse, especially Catherine Whiting, editor, and Tony Harold, managing director, for making my dream come true.

A very special thanks to Brian for his infinite love and support, both practical and emotional.

I dedicate this book to my Nan, Nellie Hawkesford.
I like to think that she is up there right now,
enjoying a gin and tonic in the Wing and a Prayer

PROLOGUE

"Sod it," said God. "I'm off."

A ring of incredulous faces stared back at Him from round the table, where the Saints were gathered together for their regular management meeting.

"What do you mean, off?" asked Saint Paul.

"I think I'm about due for a holiday, a break from these petty problems you keep expecting me to sort out. It's about time you lot showed what you're made of." He stood up.

"You can't leave us," said Peter.

"That's the thing about being omnipotent, I can do what I bloody well like," said God. And He went, leaving the Saints in a state of bewildered pique. Well, they supposed, perhaps they had taken Him a little for granted in the past, but then life at the top was easy peasy, wasn't it? Just a sleight of the hand and things were miraculously done?

CHAPTER 1

It was Tracey's first day on reception and she was waiting for a customer. "We'll throw you in at the deep end," Heather had said, "it's the only way to learn." As her immediate supervisor, Tracey had accepted that Heather ought to know best; but faced with the imminent arrival of God knew how many disorientated souls, she was fast losing her confidence. The fact was, she'd never spoken to a human being before, and today she would be one of their first points of contact.

The flash of lights and chatter of voices alerted her to the approach of one bemused coach driver and fifty-two Japanese businessmen, their state-of-the-art cameras and camcorders clicking and whirring in unison as they captured every inch of the spectacle before them. They photographed the great glass door entrance behind Tracey's desk, and the bright orange poster announcing that the establishment they were about to enter was "UNDER NEW MANAGEMENT". They photographed every detail of the sky-blue carpet and matching upholstery with the wing and cloud motifs, which were repeated in Tracey's smart new work blouse. But most of all they photographed Tracey, muttering something about her "wonderful national costume with the wings on the back".

Tracey tried to keep calm as they crowded round her desk, chattering nineteen to the dozen. She could feel her face burning with embarrassment as she made mistake after mistake entering the unspellable names onto her computer terminal. After what seemed like an eternity, she processed the last name and tapped her way through the confirmation procedure which would commit the details to the vast database.

She was just in time, for as the party disappeared behind her, another woman appeared in front. Tracey smiled sweetly as she punched in more details; name, Julia Davis, husband, Martin John Davis, dates of birth and death. She was beginning to relax now. A solitary client was easier to cope with than a whole coachload; indeed this one looked more nervous than she was; Tracey could swear she heard butterflies in the woman's stomach. Waiting for the computer to digest the details, she cast her gaze over the woman's blouse; it was pretty, the pattern and design worthy of committing to memory. Perhaps later she would reproduce it for her own wardrobe.

The computer screen flashed at her: it had found a match. Tracey pressed the key to print out the information and handed it to the smiling, grateful woman, along with a colourful folder from a pile on her desk. "Have a nice day," she said, as the woman turned to walk through the entrance doors.

Tracey returned her gaze to the screen, her finger poised above the key that would take her back to the main menu, ready for the next client. The screen was flashing again, but this time highlighting different information. Her heart missed a beat. Why hadn't she noticed that before? Oh well, it was too late now; the woman had gone and Tracey could only hope that her superiors wouldn't find out who was responsible for this terrible mistake. She pressed the return key just as Heather emerged from her office.

"Tracey, did I just see a party of Japanese arrive, or am I imagining things?"

"Yes, they've just been through."

"Where are they, then? They haven't arrived at the Housing Allocations desk. I'd better check on the computer in case they've gone to another department by mistake. She leant over Tracey's

9

shoulder, tapped at the keyboard and frowned. "That's strange, I can't seem to find their records." She continued tapping, then stood back and folded her arms. "Tracey, what have you done?"

* * *

The driver and his party walked out of the arrivals lounge to find a vast car park, empty but for one, all too familiar, vehicle. The driver turned to go back to the reception to ask for directions, but the building had disappeared. There was no option but to follow the Japanese who were now enthusiastically piling back onto the coach.

* * *

Hiram thumped the table with his fist. "We'll never get anywhere with that attitude!" he complained. "When are you guys gonna realise that you gotta move with the times?"

"There have been more than enough changes round here," said St Peter, haughtily. "And they haven't always been for the better."

St Paul nodded in agreement. "We've become too soft, too liberal. Now, if I had my way. . ."

Hiram didn't let him finish. "Yeah, Paul. We all know your views. But think now, what are we in this game for? We gotta pack 'em in, get butts on seats."

St Peter wrinkled his nose in disgust as he dug St Paul in the ribs with his bony elbow. "I said we'd rue the day we let the Yank get involved."

Hiram ignored him. "Look, you've just gone stale up here – and you're not attracting enough people."

"So you believe the answer is to lower our standards even further?"

St Peter sighed. Things really were not working out. In fact, since God had gone off in His huff – where to, only He knew –

almost everything had gone wrong. Declaring a State of Emergency, Peter and the other Saints had elected a board of Trustees, comprising Paul, John, Matthew and Luke, with himself in the Chair. But nothing had been as easy as they had believed, and they had soon worn themselves out. There were simply too many decisions to make. It had been Luke's idea to inject fresh blood into the board, to bring fresh ideas, and then, as if in answer to their prayers, along had come "Saint" Hiram P Toogood – the title had been one of his conditions of accepting the position of Chief Executive.

Peter, of course, had been against it from the start. After all, Hiram was a relative newcomer to Heaven – no matter how outstanding his track record on earth. An evangelist from Georgia, USA, he had achieved instant martyrdom on the occasion of his assassination during a sell-out appearance at the Hollywood Bowl. In spite of the hype and the multi-million business that he generated, Peter conceded, Hiram was a sincere man, a man almost bursting with goodness. He believed in the message that he spread of repentance, atonement, forgiveness and redemption. He worshipped his God, adored his wife, and loved every man, woman and child in the human race. And he still had enough love left for all creatures great and small. As a prominent religious leader, he'd been invited to a welcome reception where he'd impressed many of the saints with his progressive ideas and boundless energy. He was just the sort of man, St Luke had said, to help shoulder the responsibilities, whilst bringing a much-needed touch of modernism to the old place.

He'd certainly done that. St Peter thought wistfully of the Pearly Gates and the hosts of harp-playing angels that used to greet the newly departed. Those gates had been his domain, something he had been proud of and he had enjoyed giving a personal welcome to all the new arrivals. But it was old-fashioned, Hiram had told him; and now it had all gone. In place of the old gates was an ugly imitation of an airport terminal, all chrome and plate glass, fully

11

staffed with uniform-clad angels who provided directions, welcome packs and smiles in abundance. Peter blamed himself; he should never have let the others talk him into it. He'd protested to Hiram, of course, but his words had been dismissed with a shrug of the shoulders. "Come on, Pete old buddy, you gotta admit, it's more efficient than the old system. Remember those endless queues?"

And Hiram hadn't stopped there. He'd created a monstrous organisation to take over the day to day running of Heaven. "The art of good management," he'd told the Trustees, "is delegation."

The responsibility for processing the newly departed now came under the remit of the Information Department, which also administered the new computerised information and communication network that Hiram had installed. Peter, who had assumed that he would remain in overall charge of this function, had been horrified when Hiram had brought in Saint Martha as Director. "Needs the feminine touch," Hiram had said – "a more sympathetic approach. Besides, I think the Trust should concentrate on formulating policy and planning ahead rather than getting too involved with line management."

Then there was the Housing Department, which Peter saw no need for at all. It wasn't as if there was an accommodation problem. Up here everyone could live in the home of their dreams. But Hiram had argued that although most people had an idea of what sort of house they wanted, few could visualise it in sufficient detail to translate their dreams into a practical dwelling place. The new Housing Department published a catalogue containing designs for every imaginable type of building. People simply had to choose, and the angels would make it happen.

Neither did Peter think there was any need for a Planning Department – space, after all, was infinite. However, Hiram thought that things had been allowed to get out of hand for too long; the whole place was "higgledy-piggledy", he'd said. Vast oriental palaces sprang up among tiny thatched cottages, sprawling modern bungalows and elegant town houses – it just wasn't "aesthetically pleasing". So Hiram had asked the Department to draw up proposals to designate zones for the various types of dwellings. They liaised closely with the Housing Department in an attempt to modify some of their clients' wildest excesses. "D'ya realise," said Hiram, "that we now have at least two hundred thousand Taj Mahals dotted around the place? Letting everyone do their own thing doesn't work – we gotta give them some guidance."

Finally there was the Education and Leisure Department, which encouraged Heaven's citizens to use their time productively; to acquire knowledge and new skills. As well as academic subjects, classes were available in every imaginable leisure pursuit.

But it was all so soulless, Peter thought sadly. And now Hiram had started to talk about the next stage in his plan.

* * *

Somehow Julia Davis wasn't surprised to find a New York style taxi-cab waiting for her outside the reception building. Things had been getting better and better since her arrival in Heaven – although she was still marvelling at being here at all. The only reason she had been into a church in the last thirty or so years had been for weddings and funerals, and according to the Catholic Church, that made her a mortal sinner condemned to an eternity in Hell.

Coming through "Customs" earlier on, she had taken the red channel, defiantly declaring this and other sins, and been waved through with just a cursory nod. Over in the green channel, however, angels were swooping down on those self-righteous pillars of the community who attempted to smuggle their sins into Heaven and ushering them into a crowded waiting room where they would be left to contemplate their fate. Congratulating herself on having made the right choice, Julia had begun to feel her muscles tighten as she walked on. Liver spots on her hands faded away and the dried, wrinkled skin became soft and smooth. Her grey hair, too, scraped away from her face in the style she had kept for most of her adult life, burst free, growing dark and luxuriant over her shoulders. She had become a young woman again. Yes, Heaven was looking like a good place to be. She was surprised to find a group of young people, clutching notebooks and cameras, flocking towards her, paparazzi style, and decided that it must be a case of mistaken identity. She wasn't going to wait to find out, she had other priorities.

Julia stepped into the taxi and handed over the address she had been given at reception to the driver: 107,378, Five Million and Thirty Second Street, Elysian Fields, Heaven 17. Her feelings were mixed: on the one hand, she couldn't wait to get to her destination and be reunited with her husband; on the other, she felt nervous, sure that she would break down and cry with the emotion of it all. And then there was Martin, would he be how she remembered him?

"How long will it take to get there?" she asked the driver.

"No time at all, sweetheart," he said, smiling back at her. "I don't suppose you've had time to look at your welcome pack yet?"

"No," said Julia, glancing down at the colourful folder on her lap.

"Probably a good thing. It's not exactly what I'd call light reading. But it does explain the way things work round here. I can't say I understand all the why's and wherefore's, but I can try to put a few things in layman's terms if you like."

"Yes please," said a confused Julia.

"It's like this. Events here happen consecutively and concurrently at the same time, if you get my drift. It's something to do with everything happening simultaneously, but you experience them in sequence, because that's what you're used to."

"I think I understand," said Julia, thinking that she didn't understand at all and that perhaps she had better read the welcome pack anyway.

"The good thing about it," he continued, "is that everything you do, everything that happens to you, will take exactly as long as you want it to. Take me and the missus, it's like us going on holiday. Now, her idea of fun is to lie all day on a beach, soaking up the sun, but that bores me stupid. I like going out for long walks, soaking up the scenery. In Heaven, that beach holiday will seem like it's lasting a lifetime to my missus, while the same holiday to me will pass in the blink of an eye. The same thing goes for my walking holiday but the other way round. So, we both get what we want without the other having to suffer."

"I see," said Julia. "It's like the opposite to Earth, where time flies when you're enjoying yourself and drags if you're bored."

"That's it. You've got the idea. Take this journey for another example. If we hadn't have had this little conversation, or if you hadn't been interested in what we've been talking about, you'd have arrived at your destination immediately."

Julia realised with surprise that she had been totally unaware of the journey itself, outside their conversation. If there had been any scenery, she'd missed it completely. The cabby seemed to glean her thoughts.

"We needn't arrive yet. If you want to take a bit longer, it's all right by me."

She smiled at him. "No, I think I'm ready now, thanks." No sooner had she finished speaking when the cab glided to a halt outside a small terraced house. Julia thanked the cabby and stepped out onto the sparkling pavement. She checked the house number, 107,378, yes, this was it, although she was surprised that Martin had chosen to live in a poky little place like this rather than the smart, modern detached house where they'd spent their short married life.

Almost tearful with anticipated joy, Julia rang the doorbell. The door opened immediately, and a shocked Julia found herself facing a woman whom she'd seen only in photographs. Lucy, Martin's first wife, who'd died before Julia had met him.

* * *

"What on earth's going on in reception?" asked St James, Director of Housing. "There's a woman crying. For Christ's sake, people are supposed to be happy around here."

"There's been another fuck-up in the Information Department," Mary Magdalene explained, her husky voice sending shivers down St James's spine. "It's that bird-brain Tracey again – forgot to tell some poor woman that her beloved husband was shacked up with his first wife."

"Don't tell me, this wouldn't be the same angel who managed to lose an entire coachload of Japanese?"

She nodded.

"I hate to have to say it," said James who, on the contrary, was obviously enjoying every moment, "but Martha just can't hack it as a Director. She's far too soft with those angels of hers. I put it down to the millennia she spent looking after the babies in Limbo. I said as much to Peter at the time, I said . . ."

"Oh, put a sock in it, James. You're not so bloody infallible. Who was the one who built the housing estate for pacifists right next door to Valhalla? Let he who is without sin cast the first stone?" With a contemptuous toss of her untamed mane of black hair, Mary Magdalene flounced out of the office.

St James shook his head. This idea of Hiram's to give the women more responsibility just wasn't working. James had been horrified when he'd heard that Mary Magdalene was to be his deputy. He was a firm believer in the idea that fallen women never quite regained an upright position. Maggie had the look of a woman who would fall again at the slightest nudge. But what really infuriated

16

him was that she had absolutely no respect for his rank and didn't bother to pretend otherwise.

* * *

Maggie sat Julia Davis down in a comfy chair in reception and offered her a cigarette.

"It must have been a terrible shock for you," she said, sympathetically. "I know it probably won't help, but there are many others in your position. Unfortunately, we've never been able to sort out the dilemma of what to do about second and successive husbands and wives, and we've had a few upset by it recently."

"I'd forgotten all about her," sniffed Julia, waving away the cigarette. "We'd only been married a few months when Martin died and he was always so tactful. He hardly mentioned her at all to me. And then coming up here, in the excitement I never stopped to think."

Sniffs became sobs as she thought of the thirty years she'd spent as a widow, worshipping the memory of her late husband and wanting no other; comforted only by the thought of their eventual reunion. It had been so wonderful to find herself in Heaven, a young woman again with everything to look forward to. Then had come that dreadful moment at the house when, looking past Lucy she had seen Martin, a look of guilt and embarrassment spreading over his face. How she'd found her way to the Housing Department in this state, she had no idea.

"Our first priority is to get you settled," said Maggie, adopting an efficient tone of voice. "We've got a temporary hostel where you can stay until you decide what to do. You shouldn't be on your own at a time like this and at least there'll be other people there for you to talk to. Don't despair. There's an organisation up here who are fighting for fair treatment for people in your situation. They'll be in touch very soon."

17

Maggie stood up and ushered Julia outside and into another taxi cab; then returned to her desk, sighing. The institution of marriage had recently started to create a whole host of problems. In the beginning God had said that there was no need for marriage in Heaven; that spirits should just float about in the ether, blissfully happy with their new-found freedom. But even the first generation of arrivals had clung to the symbols of their Earthly existence, refusing to be happy unless they were reunited with their loved ones. Until recently this had operated happily enough on a strictly "first come, first served" basis, but since the advent of Hiram and his installation of untrained angels on the reception desk, there had been more than a few complaints about "unfair treatment".

* * *

Tracey stared down at the carpet, her eyes following the outlines of the harps and clouds in an attempt not to cry.

"I'm at my wits' end." The Archangel Raphael shook his head. "I just don't know what to do with you. You've been expelled from the School for Guardian Angels, thrown out of the Heavenly Choir and now sacked from the Information Department. You've broken one of our cardinal rules by making a new citizen unhappy and, if that wasn't bad enough, there's a whole coachload of arrivals gone missing. God knows where they've got to." He reached behind his desk for something. Tracey peeped out from under her lashes as the Archangel held out a sweeping brush. "I'm afraid it's cloud cleaning for you."

* * *

The only exit from the car park led to a highway which seemed to provide nowhere for the coach to stop. There were no lay-bys, no car parks and no exits. For the Japanese businessmen, this was not a problem. From the comfort of their seats on the luxury coach, they could marvel at the varied and magnificent dwellings which lined the streets, the exotic vegetation of the botanical gardens which replicated every type of habitation they had ever seen, and more, and the herds of what they had believed to be extinct and mythological beasts roaming the grounds of somewhere called Saint Francis' Zoo and Safari Park.

All in all they were delighted with this unscheduled addition to their tour and kept telling each other that they'd recommend this company to their friends as soon as they got back home. The driver, on the other hand, was not a happy man. He was envisaging an eternity spent on the coach, and he drove like a demon in search of an escape route. Then at last, in the near distance, a turn-off materialised: a small retail and leisure development comprising an arcade of souvenir shops, a large hotel and a club billed as "Valhalla – The Best Nite Spot Ever". A poster at the entrance offered them all that they could eat and drink, served by beautiful, blonde wenches. The driver sighed with relief as he pulled the coach to a halt and the Japanese poured out, intent on an endless night of drunken debauchery, doubtless followed by a mega Valhalla-sized hangover. But no, they were not going to leave him alone. Three of them were returning to drag him off to alcoholic oblivion with them. It was just such oblivion that had put them in this mess in the first place, he thought resentfully, at last remembering the warning signposts for the unfinished motorway bridge that had caught his eye moments before he lost consciousness.

* * *

"Let me run this past you," Hiram was saying to the Trustees, who were listening in disbelief. "How long is it since you last carried out a marketing exercise – you know, really pulled out the stops to promote this place?"

"I resent that," said St Peter. "I think that the churches have been doing their damnedest over the years. I won't hear a word said against them."

"Hey, back down, Pete," said Hiram. "You're preaching to the converted, remember? After all, I was one of your best ambassadors on Earth. I worked my butt off to get the message across, but Hell, I reckon I was pissing into the wind most of the time. No, I'm talking about putting on a really big show. I reckon two thousand years is too long to go without a major gig."

Peter's mouth was open. "You don't mean . . . ?"

"Yeah. You got it, pal. We need the big J.C. to make His comeback."

"On the Oprah Winfrey Show, I suppose?" enquired St Paul.

"Hey man, I reckon you're tuning in to my wavelength at last."

"You can't be serious," said St John.

"Just think about it. It's only the twentieth century equivalent of Jesus doing His stuff in the temple or the Sermon on the Mount. It's all about communication. I'm sure J.C. would see the logic in that."

"I think he's got a point," said Luke. "It's a case of having to adapt ourselves to present conditions. After all, that's why we brought Hiram in. The least we can do is to give his proposal serious consideration."

"I second that," said St Matthew. "It's a long time since any of us were down there. Things have changed."

"I'm not allowing us to be railroaded into any rash decisions," said St Peter. "But if Hiram wants to go away and draw up a detailed scheme then I suppose the least we can do is look at it. But remember, we're not the only ones who'll have to be convinced. You're going to have to come up with something good if you expect God to agree to it, especially in His present mood." God had, at last, sent them a forwarding address on a postcard. Apparently, He was soaking up the sun in the desert of some planet in the galaxy of Andromeda, but had absolutely no wish for any of them to be there too – except in strict cases of emergency.

"You're right there," agreed Matthew. "He's made it quite clear that He doesn't want to be disturbed."

"So, if you're all agreed," said Peter, "we'll adjourn the meeting to give Hiram time to prepare a full report."

* * *

"Fancy a pint?" asked Paul, as they left the meeting.

"I think we've earned one," said Peter. "The Wing as usual?"

The lounge of the Wing and a Prayer was full. In truth, it was always full as it adjusted its size according to the number of customers present at any one time. The floor of the pub appeared to be made from clouds, the ceiling from a sky crammed with twinkling stars and streaked with comets. The walls looked solid enough until you tried to examine them closely, at which point they would just dissolve into mist. In one corner, a pretty blonde angel plucked at her harp. There were no bottles, no barrels, just a single tap from which the barman dispensed water which would transform into the drink of the customer's choice.

The pub was open to all, but in practice was only patronised by the angels and saints. The ordinary citizens of Heaven preferred the Gate and Trumpet which had a juke box stocked with every record ever released and, more importantly, boasted a dartboard and pool table.

Peter nodded to a couple of Archangels who were seated at a table. They glared back.

"What's up with those two?" Paul asked him as they carried their pints of Old Celestial to their usual table.

"I don't know. It seems that a lot of old resentments have been coming to the surface recently."

"You don't reckon God's gone for good?"

"I shouldn't imagine so. Remember He did this to us once on

21

Earth?" Peter picked up his glass and took a mouthful. "No, I reckon He'll be back soon. If I know Him, He's probably trying to teach us some sort of lesson. Not that He hasn't earned a rest, I think we've all realised what hard work it is running this Kingdom. Fancy a scratching?" He offered the bag to Paul.

"Thanks. In the meantime, what do you propose to do about Hiram?"

Peter waited until he'd finished crunching before speaking. "I don't know what I can do really. We agreed from the start that the Trust would be run democratically, I can hardly start throwing my weight about now, just because I don't agree with a decision."

"But you heard him at the meeting, the man's a nutter."

"Exactly. And if the others can't see that now, they soon will when he presents his report. If what he's come up with so far is anything to go by, he's not going to need any help from us to show how ridiculous his ideas are. The Oprah Winfrey show, indeed!"

"I hope you're right, but you've seen the way Luke looks at him, as if the sun shines out of his backside. And Matthew is bound to agree with Luke, he always does."

"We'll have to see. In the meantime I'll try to have a quiet word with John. To tell you the truth, I was a bit surprised when he voted to appoint Hiram, I thought he had more sense." He drained his pint. "Fancy another? I'll get them in."

* * *

A pair of hooded eyes watched the two saints from another table. "Just look at them, they think they're so bloody important," mumbled the Archangel Gabriel to Michael over his pint of Heavenly Oblivion, the strongest brew in the house. "Them and that Hiram Toogood. Why is it, do you think, we're never the ones to be rewarded with any respect and authority round here. After all the dirty work we do for them! I can tell you, it took a lot of tact and diplomacy to tell a pious little virgin in Nazareth that she was up the spout by the Holy Ghost. Then I have to go and explain things to her betrothed – that was tricky, believe me. And in return, do we get appointed on any Board of Trustees? Do we Hell."

"Yeah!" agreed Michael, caught up in the spirit of their oppression. Gabriel downed his pint, lurched from his seat and staggered out of the pub, followed closely by Michael, their swaying wings sweeping glasses from several tables as they passed.

The Angel Tracey appeared with her brush and started to sweep up the mess.

* * *

"I thought you'd have wanted me to be happy," said Martin.

"You marry another woman barely six months after my death and you expect my blessing?" Lucy was weeping and wailing and gnashing her teeth while Martin looked pleadingly at her. "Why didn't you tell me before, why did you let me find out like this?"

"It was difficult," said Martin, slowly. "When I arrived, I thought you'd know already, but when I realised you didn't, well, I was so happy to see you again that I didn't want to spoil things. Then I just sort of forgot about her."

Lucy sat down. She remembered her own arrival in Heaven, how she'd missed Martin, and her surprise that she was unable to watch over him. Then after a little while, she'd forgotten all about him, until he turned up on her doorstep.

It always came as a surprise to newcomers that they were cut off in this way from the people they'd left behind. In fact, it wasn't impossible to make contact: with determination and some imagination, the veil that separated the two dominions could be penetrated, but this was not encouraged. In most cases, it wasn't long before new residents were blessed with a forgetfulness which prevented them from pining for, or worrying about, their loved ones. This process was usually painless and passed unnoticed. One moment the newcomer would be fondly remembering darling Fred or Mary, the next, gently struggling to put names to vague faces, then soon after the memories would vanish completely. The gaps left would be filled by the wonders of Heaven or by the joy of reunion with old friends and relatives. Until, that is, their loved ones joined them. That was when the trouble started for people like Martin, Lucy and Julia.

Encouraged by Lucy's thoughtful silence, Martin reached for her hand, but she snatched it away and walked to the window. After a few moments she spoke, calmly and slowly. "You should have told me about her in the first place. Well, now you can move into the spare room while I think what to do."

"But we haven't got a spare room."

"We have now." Lucy had not been idle during the last few moments; she had been carrying out a few alterations to the house and there was indeed a new feature, a poky little box room with a single bed, which Lucy had thoughtfully equipped with a particularly lumpy mattress and nylon sheets. She knew that Martin would be able to make it more comfortable, but she wanted to show him the full extent of her anger.

* * *

They'd filmed and photographed every inch of the hotel and found that it had everything they could possibly ask for: en-suite facilities with non-adjustable showerheads that projected powerful horizontal jets of water; tiny tablets of soap that refused to lather; damp towels that were refolded daily but rarely replaced. And they could never be sure that there was enough toilet paper to last until the next day. Then there were the tea-making facilities: tiny kettles that took half an hour to boil, strictly rationed sachets of tea, coffee and sugar, postage stamp-size biscuits wrapped in cellophane, plastic juglets of milk and half-cream, replenished daily. The restaurant had always finished serving hot breakfasts five minutes before the guests arrived. And back in the bedrooms, the heating was full on and none of the windows would open.

It had been perfect, agreed the Japanese, as they piled onto the coach, ready for the next stage of the tour. Quite perfect.

CHAPTER 2

If the angels and saints had been restless lately, this was due, not only to the absence of God, but also to an element of culture shock. Hiram had made a lot of changes, and they hadn't been incremental. In Heaven, as soon as people made up their minds what they wanted, it would happen almost instantaneously. There were no long waits while the plans were drawn up by the architect and approved by planning committees, while the contractor chased the suppliers, while the building work was delayed by the weather. Up in Heaven, no sooner had the word been said than the deed was done. That is, as long as the angels weren't taking industrial action.

Even before he'd reorganised the reception and set up the departments, Hiram had been busy. One of his first moves was to abolish two long-standing institutions: Limbo and Purgatory.

As far as Limbo was concerned, Hiram said it was outdated and draconian; after all, it was hardly the fault of the unbaptised infants or the people who'd lived and died before Christ that they were in that situation. So Limbo had been closed without further ado and its inmates, after a suitable period of induction, assimilated into Heaven. Or so Hiram had planned. They stuck out a mile, these new citizens. The Old Testament prophets stumbled round the place in a state of shock and the babies, artificially accelerated to adulthood, were prone to plonking themselves down in the most awkward of places, filling their nappies, sticking their thumbs in

26

their mouths and wailing for their next feed.

Then Hiram had turned his attention to Purgatory, where those who had died with relatively minor sins on their souls did a little "time" before being released into Heaven. Hiram decided that the emphasis should be on rehabilitation rather than punishment, so he closed Purgatory down and replaced it with a scheme of community service. The sinners were now put to good use for an appropriate period; sweeping the streets and clouds, helping to muck out the cages at St Francis' Zoo and Safari Park or cleaning up after the Limbo babies.

To signal this spirit of liberality, Hiram erected a new sign at the entrance to Heaven:

WELCOME

Although this is Christian Heaven, we welcome people
regardless of race, colour, gender, creed, age, disability
and sexual orientation. (As long as they've been good
boys and girls, of course!)
Heaven – Working Towards Equal Opportunities

This came as something of a shock to those whose religions preached that theirs was the only, narrow path to Heaven, that any who fell by the wayside would be cast down into the depths of Hell. Even more shocked were those who were convinced that there was no after-life. They usually went into trauma immediately on arrival.

The New Limbo Hostel for the Temporarily Displaced was the resting place for many of these poor, dazed souls until they recovered from their shock. Other residents included former inmates of Limbo and Purgatory, some of whom were eternally institutionalised, victims of violent death, and, recently, men and women who, like Julia, were prevented from joining their spouses.

Julia had been shown to a charming little bedroom in the hostel.

"I should read your welcome pack first," the kindly warden had advised. "Then perhaps you'd like to come down to the common room and meet some of the others." So Julia sat on her bed skimming through the Citizen's Guide that was included in the welcome pack, along with an enamel badge, a pen and a car sticker.

INTRODUCTION

This Citizen's Guide is intended only as a brief user-friendly guide to Heaven. Should any citizens wish to study any particular area in more detail, they are welcome to ask one of the angels, who are always willing to help and to advise, or consult the infinite number of volumes on any conceivable subject that are available in the Paradise Library.

She skipped the lengthy and complicated section about the peculiar properties of time and space in Heaven, grateful for the taxi driver's simple explanation.

The guide also contained information on the comprehensive services provided by a host of trained angels and tips on where to find the best pint of beer and tastiest fish and chips. It told her that, whilst it was possible for citizens to create their own buildings and environments, there was no need; that was what the angels were for. The section entitled "The Social Scene" made her suddenly wish for company and, after freshening herself up, she went downstairs.

The term "common room" had been something of an understatement, thought Julia, as she gazed out over an endless sea of people. Although they all seemed to be talking at once, the noise was surprisingly low and rather pleasant. As Julia stood uncertainly in the doorway, she noticed a woman approaching. "Hello, I'm Cathy," the woman said. "Come in, I'll introduce you to the others." Her smile was warm and friendly and Julia felt as if she'd always known her.

"The others?"

"Sorry, I should have said. I'm a founder member of S.P.O.R.R., the Society for the Promotion of Rights for the Remarried."

"Oh, yes. The lady at the Housing Department did mention something."

"That'll be Maggie, she's sympathetic towards our organisation, even though she's never been married. She isn't really supposed to give us publicity, we're considered to be rather anti-establishment." She beamed proudly. "I'm responsible for new members."

Cathy led Julia to an area of the room where chairs were set out in an immense spiral around a centre table, spinning out further than the eye could see. A countless number of men and women were filing into the seats with, considering the numbers involved, a remarkable speed and lack of collisions. Cathy led Julia to a seat near the inner edge of the spiral.

"It must be a nightmare to organise a meeting this size," sympathised Julia, who had spent several years working for a company that organised seminars and conferences.

"On the contrary," Cathy said, "there's no problem at all. The meeting is held, and everyone who wants to attend comes at a point in time that is convenient to them. It's impossible to be late for a meeting in Heaven." By the time she had finished speaking, everyone was in their seats, including the officials who sat at the centre table.

Copies of a petition calling for equal rights for all spouses were being circulated and soon materialised on Julia's lap. She signed it and then handed it to the next person.

Julia was surprised by the variety of people there. Judging by her own personal experience, and from the people she'd seen so far, she'd assumed that everyone would look approximately the same age, in their twenties or thirties. She found it hard to believe that so many people had elected to appear as they had in their forties, fifties and, in quite a few cases, even older. The range of races, colours and historical periods represented was similarly remarkable. It was as if she'd stumbled on a combined dress rehearsal for every costume drama or travel documentary ever made.

Cathy noticed Julia's look of amazement. "It does rather take your breath away, doesn't it?" She drew Julia's attention to some of the more interesting members. There were five of Henry VIII's wives, all in Tudor costume. "Catherine of Aragon was delighted to have him back."

"I'm surprised that the others want a share, after the way he treated them." Julia watched the five women laughing happily together. She noticed how two of them seemed to hold their heads rather stiffly.

"Oh, Henry's no danger up here. I've heard that he's mellowed considerably, he's quite the new man now." Cathy turned her attention to a rather distinguished looking man sitting next to a young woman who was biting her fingernails. "That's Max and his second wife, can't for the life of me remember her name. Now, his first wife, Rebecca, she's a real beauty, in fact, she's probably here somewhere." She craned her neck, scanning the endless rows of people. "Yes, do you see that woman with the black hair? That's Rebecca." She lowered her whisper even further. "He killed her, you know."

"A murderer, here?"

"Don't look so surprised, he repented of course, but just imagine their shock when they were reunited. Oh, the meeting's starting now."

As Julia listened to the points made by various speakers, agreeing whole-heartedly with their sentiments, she was surprised to find a piece of paper landing in her lap. It was a note from the warden, telling her that a gentleman was in reception, asking to see her.

* * *

30

Since Julia had presented herself at his door, Martin had tried to talk to Lucy, but she remained intent on conspicuously ignoring him. He had done everything he could think of to make amends, conjuring up bouquets of flowers and "Sorry" cards with cute pictures of bunnies. Lucy just withered his flowers and set the cards ablaze with one flash of her eyes. In the end he had retreated to his room to sulk, leaving her to her favourite soap opera.

For the first time since seeing her again, Martin allowed himself to think of Julia. Their marriage had been tragically cut short before the bliss of the honeymoon phase had been overtaken by reality. Their happiness had never been blighted by a cross word or an angry look. Although he had been happy with Lucy, he was gradually remembering certain things that had grated in the past: her quick temper and biting sarcasm, the way she had criticised him in front of friends.

Both women had suffered, he realised, but at this moment his sympathies were with Julia. Bewildered and no doubt friendless in a strange place, she had been let down badly by the very person she had relied on. Silently, Martin slipped downstairs and out of the house into a waiting taxi. In no time at all he was standing in the reception of the New Limbo Hostel, and Julia was walking towards him.

She looked exactly as she had done when they'd been together on Earth: slim and pretty, with long, dark hair and large, soft brown eyes, her skin pale, her lips slightly parted. He'd forgotten how much like Lucy she looked, but, after all, that was what had attracted him to her in the first place.

Julia did what she had longed to do for thirty years: she ran to him and flung herself into his arms. "You've left her?"

"Er, no, not exactly," said Martin. "I sort of . . . slipped out. I had to see you."

Julia disentangled herself from his arms and stood back. "You sort of slipped out?" Suddenly she looked exactly like Lucy. "Who

31

do you think I am? I'm your wife, not some cheap little tart that you're seeing on the side." Julia couldn't believe what she was saying after spending half her life pining for this man.

"Things are different up here, darling. It's so complicated."

"All the more reason why we should sort it out. What do we do now, shall I come back with you and the three of us can sit down and discuss it?"

Martin's eyes widened in what looked suspiciously like fear, even horror. "No, we can't do that, it's too soon, Lucy would throw a fit." He added – too quickly, Julia thought – "Perhaps we could meet here? No need for Lucy to know, until the time is right."

"Oh, we mustn't upset poor Lucy, must we. It doesn't matter about me, as long as the lovely Lucy is happy."

"Please, darling. You must understand how difficult this is for me."

Julia's eyes narrowed. Now, as she looked at him, it was as if she was seeing the real Martin for the first time: weak and self-centred. She thought of those other couples at the meeting, second partners grasping at stolen moments with their loved ones, and decided that it wasn't going to be like that for her, not when she wasn't sure whether the prize was worth the contest. She'd wasted the best part of her life yearning for Martin and she wasn't going to compromise by settling for second best. She was worth more than that. "No," she said firmly. "On the contrary, I think you've had things too easy, for a long, long time. I'm not prepared to accept the leftovers from Lucy's table. As far as I'm concerned, you can rot in Heaven together." She turned and walked away.

* * *

Hiram hadn't expected it to be like this. It wasn't unlike Earth, with ordinary streets, ordinary people going about their business, albeit a little hungover, judging by the look of them. He didn't look down at the pavement. If he had, he might have noticed that it was neatly laid out in little cobbles, in the form of letters, spelling out, again and again, the words "Good Intentions". It was one of Satan's little jokes.

The invitation he'd received had been strangely irresistible; it had started to smoulder the instant it landed in his in-tray. Hiram had picked it up and dropped it just as quickly, for it was edged with fire and hot to the touch.

> HIS SATANIC MAJESTY cordially invites
> HIRAM P TOOGOOD to visit him in Hell
> Dress – Smoking Jacket (optional)

Peter and the other saints had tried to discourage him. "It's horrible down there," they'd said. "Hot. And smelly. You'll probably be tortured."

But Hiram just shook his head. He liked to think of himself as a strategist, and he always made it part of his strategy to get to know the opposition.

Before he left, the others had decked him with charms: crucifixes concealed in the pockets of his clothing; an angel's feather sewn into the hem of his jacket; even a necklace of garlic bulbs. "Superstitious mumbo jumbo," he'd said. The others looked worried.

"But you must believe in them," they'd said, "otherwise they won't work."

After practically drowning Hiram in Holy Water, Peter had called after him, "Don't forget, you mustn't eat or drink anything while you're down there, or you'll be stuck there for eternity."

Hiram smelt the musky, sulphurous stench of the place, felt its heat, before he saw it. "The Hellfire Club (The Original)" the sign proclaimed, its entrance a flaming mouth leading to a dark cave. Inside, a smiling, exceptionally good looking demon, who introduced himself as Jake, led Hiram through a mass of writing bodies which parted to let him pass untouched. As he followed the demon, Hiram caught sight of a blackboard, fixed to the wall. Words were burnt into it, and, as far as Hiram could make out, were still burning.

HELL'S KITCHEN
TODAY'S MENU
Devils on Horseback Devilled Chicken Shrimp Diabolo
Devil's Food Cake

Hiram was reassured; at least the Devil appeared to have a sense of humour. With a chuckle he recognised the music that pulsated around him, the Stones' Sympathy for the Devil. Hiram was led to a table where a dark young man rose and in perfect synchronisation with the music, said, "Please allow me to introduce myself . . ."

Hiram couldn't help laughing as he shook the Devil's hand.

"I must apologise," said Satan, "but as you have probably gathered, I just can't resist the literal, the theatrical." He snapped his fingers and an attractive female demon appeared, her pen poised over an order pad. "Can I tempt you with something – a drink?"

"No, thank you kindly." Hiram remembered Peter's warning with a shudder.

"Shame on you," said the Devil. "You've been listening to those old saints' tales, haven't you? It's only a myth, you know, an old Greek legend." He patted an evil-looking poodle that shuffled up beside him. "Say hello to the nice man, Cerberus. They used to call me Pluto, you know, the Ancient Greeks." He turned back to Hiram. "It was a name I was rather fond of, until your fellow countryman used it for a cartoon dog. Still, I won't hold it against you. Something to eat then, maybe? A pomegranate?" He smiled sweetly.

"No, really, I get heartburn if I eat between meals."

"I understand, I'm not offended by your declining my hospitality." Satan clicked his fingers again and the demon waitress vanished.

34

"Really, it's just too good of you to come. Too good! Oh, no pun intended, I promise, Mr Toogood."

"No need to stand on ceremony, just call me Hiram."

"Well, thank you, Hiram, and you must call me Satan. As I was about to say, Hiram, I really appreciate the fact that you've come calling at all." The Devil had started to affect a Southern drawl. "Yo' sure yo' won't try a piece of my home-baked devil's food cake?" He fluttered his eyelashes and waved his hand in front of his face. "My, my, it sure is hot, ain't it?" Seeing Hiram's puzzled face, he giggled helplessly. "I'm sorry, Hiram, I just can't resist trying out my acting skills. The Abyss Theatre is putting on a production of Gone With The Wind – The Musical, and I'm going to be Miss Scarlett. I'll make sure you get a front seat ticket."

While Satan recovered from his fit of hysterics, Hiram took the opportunity to scrutinise him. He really was the most beautiful young man that he had ever laid eyes on and Hiram was somewhat disturbed to find himself rather attracted. He shuffled uncomfortably and tried hard to concentrate on an image of his beautiful wife, Pammy. Although he prided himself on being tolerant of other people's sexual preferences, Hiram had never before been tempted to swing both ways. He noticed the Devil's enigmatic smile: it was as if he could read every unwelcome thought that flashed through his mind. Or, more probably, as if he had put the thoughts there in the first place. Hiram became aware that another being had joined them, a heavily made up demon with pierced nipples, who wore fishnet tights and a leather jockstrap, and simpered and giggled as he stroked the Devil's thigh. He raised his arched eyebrows mockingly as he watched Hiram blush.

"Hiya, my name's Mephistopheles."

The Devil pushed the demon's hand away and spoke more seriously, his voice now that of a cultured Englishman. "You must wonder why I've asked you up here."

Hiram cleared his throat. "Well, Satan old buddy, I must admit

I'm rather curious."

The Devil made a grimace at Hiram's over familiar address. "You're not the only one. I've been asking myself why they've brought you in as – how do they describe it, Chief Executive?"

"Well, it's like this, Satan. They, that is, God wanted to bring the place up to date." Hiram was conscious of the importance of keeping God's absence a secret from the Devil.

"Don't insult our intelligence," Satan snapped. For a few moments, his voice resounded with the echo of a multitude of tongues as he leaned forward menacingly and spoke into Hiram's ear. "I know exactly where God is." He sat back and smiled, the charming host once again. "So the saints have at last come down from their pedestals and admitted they need fresh ideas? I've always made it my business to keep up with the latest trends but that lot up there have always thought themselves too high and mighty to associate with the hoi-polloi." He paused, enquiringly. "So what big project have they brought you in for? The Second Coming? Judgement Day?"

Hiram shook his head. For the first time in his life he was lost for words.

"Come on, loosen up a bit, Hiram old buddy, then perhaps we can have some fun. We could work together on this project of yours. After all, Good needs Evil to show it up in its true light."

Hiram cleared his throat again. The heat, the smoke and the smell of sulphur had made his mouth dry and at that moment he could almost have sold his soul for a glass of water. "I don't think so." He looked into the Devil's deep, dark eyes and saw a multitude of lost souls glaring back at him. He is not one man, thought Hiram.

The Devil caught the fleeting thought. "You're right," he said, his voice thickening again. "I am Legion."

"British or French Foreign?" quipped Mephistopheles.

With a resounding slap, Satan sent him spinning into the darkness. "Stupid little bugger, he has no sense of timing."

Hiram was suddenly aware that the background noise had increased to an uncomfortable level. Drum beats merged with rhythmic chants and screams of torment.

"I'm so sorry about this racket, it's pandemonium down here." The Devil summoned Jake, who whispered in his ear. "Of course, I had quite forgot. Tonight is another one of Baron Samedi's voodoo stag nights." His manner changed, as if he wanted to be buddies again. "You're welcome to join in, they always lay on a wonderful spread, barbecued chicken, goat, perhaps even something more exotic?" The Devil raised his eyebrows as a woman's scream pierced the darkness.

Hiram stood up. "It's been very . . . interesting meeting you, but I guess I'd better take my leave now."

"Oh, so soon?" The Devil pouted. "Well, you must come back again and see me sometime. Are you sure I can't get you a drink? You must be very thirsty."

In spite of his now raging thirst, Hiram declined. He just wanted to get out of this hellish place without delay.

He was waved off by the Devil and Mephistopheles who, slightly concussed, grinned cross-eyed at him. "Don't forget to come to our musical," the Devil called after him. "I'll make sure to send you tickets for the first night."

* * *

The Trustees had been anxiously awaiting Hiram's return.

"He'll never get out of there," said Peter. "And even if he does, surely this foolhardy escapade proves that he's not in his right mind. You know what they say, 'Fools rush in where angels fear to tread'."

"I agree," said Paul. "He's too reckless, too impetuous to be entrusted with an important job like this."

"But that's what makes him so perfect," argued Luke. "He's not interested in doing things the old way just because 'that's the way we've always done them'."

"I'm with Luke," said Matthew. "He reminds me of what Jesus was like when we first met him, not afraid to challenge the establishment."

"Yes, but don't forget he's not Jesus, he's not God. He's human and that means he's not infallible," warned Peter.

"He's coming," said Matthew. They could just make out the figure of Hiram in the distance. They looked at each other, then hurriedly removed the nervous expressions from their faces. They each had their own private memories of visits to Hell.

John almost broke into a sweat. He had looked forward to a meeting of minds, a battle on a philosophical level between two intellectual giants on opposite sides and he'd had no doubt that Good would triumph. It had ended with total humiliation, intellectual annihilation, as the Devil ran cerebral rings round him, tied him in verbal knots and left him feeling like a child. It had been a while until he had recovered his faith in his spiritual judgement and confidence in his intellectual abilities.

Luke felt sickened by the memory of how the Devil had led him though a moral maze, questioning his liberal ideas and revealing hidden prejudices against the very people whose rights he professed to fight for.

Satan had quickly fixed on Paul's chauvinistic attitude to women, and had accused him of having an inferiority complex. "You're scared of them, aren't you, because you know they're cleverer than you." He had burst into song "'Anything you can do, they can do better . . .'"

Matthew's humiliation was that he hadn't been invited to Hell at all. In fact, the Devil had sent him a message stating quite clearly that he didn't think him worth wasting his time. He called him a "jumped-up tax collector whose only claim to fame was a gospel that had been copied from somebody else". Matthew hadn't told the other saints about the message and when, from time to time, they speculated about the fact that he'd never been there, he'd just say, "Well, it's obvious that he's too afraid of me." And he would cross his fingers, hoping that they'd never find out the truth, but he knew as sure as Exodus is Exodus that one day the Devil would reveal the truth in spectacular and embarrassing fashion for all to see: a burning sign in the sky, perhaps, or a front page article in *The Herald*. The Devil's real intention was altogether more subtle and cruel: he would just let Matthew wait in tortured anticipation, for eternity.

Peter's weak spot had been an obvious one. The Devil had laughed at him. "You've come here expecting fire and brimstone and slow, exquisite torture, but I don't need to go to that trouble, do I?" At that point, Peter had heard a cock crow. "Why do they call you the rock? If we sliced you in half, would we find the word coward running all the way through?" The cock had crowed twice. "You're a coward, Peter, you disowned your God and would probably disown your own mother." And the cock had crowed three times.

They had all survived their encounters with the Devil but only, they thought, because of their sainthood. Each had privately been convinced that Hiram would not return.

Now he was near enough for them to see that, although a little red in the face, he was otherwise apparently undamaged by his adventure. By the time he reached the saints, they were all smiling and laughing.

"Have a good trip, Hiram?" Peter laughed and slapped him on the back.

"Yeah. You know, you guys nearly had me going with all your talk of torture, but he's just a pussycat, isn't he?" No way was Hiram going to admit how much he had been rattled.

"Absolutely," said John. "A mere lightweight."

"Somewhat capricious," said Hiram, "but amusing."

"I suppose he's invited you to one of his musicals?" asked Peter. "We went to the opening night of Godspell. You wouldn't believe how dire it was. The Devil played Jesus and a mincing Mephistopheles was Mary Magdalene. It was so bad, we had to laugh. Didn't we, lads?" The others laughed on cue.

They carried on laughing and joking, just a little too loud, a little too heartily, as they walked back to their headquarters in the civic offices.

* * *

Mary Magdalene lit a cigarette and took a drag; she was tapping impatiently on the table top with her perfectly manicured talons. "You're letting me down, Martha. You're letting us all down."

St Martha stared miserably into her cold coffee. "But I'm not happy. I just can't cope. I shall be ill if I go on much longer."

"Your trouble," said Maggie, "is that you have no confidence in your own abilities. You can do this job, Martha, as good as, and a damn sight better than, most men."

Martha's mouth was set in an uncharacteristically stubborn manner. "But I don't want to."

Maggie was firm. "If you quit now, you'll be handing it to them on a plate. 'We were right all along,' they'll say. Come on, Martha, you know how long we've fought to break through the glass ceiling."

"But I felt safer, happier under the shelter of that glass. They should have made you a director instead of me."

"I agree," Maggie snapped. "But they didn't, did they? I'm too much of a rebel, too much of a threat. We haven't made it yet, not by a long chalk. But I'll be damned if I let you ruin it at this stage." She stubbed out her cigarette. "What we really need is a woman on the Trust, so we can have a real say in how this place is run. Then, and only then, you'll be able to fade into the background and concentrate on your knitting, if that's what you really want." She

40

stood up and walked out of the Ambrosia Coffee Bar, a thousand pairs of eyes watching her.

Mary Magdalene was a walking paradox: a saint with a body made for sin. She sashayed through Heaven in tight dresses, with necklines provocatively low and hemlines dangerously high, trailing clouds of musk from the perfumed oil that she used to anoint her body and dress her untameable curls. Even the most celibate saints sighed as she passed by; then later they would complain that her dress, her demeanour was unbecoming for one in her position. "For God's sake, woman, wear a veil," they said. Maggie would just laugh. "I'll wear what I like, I dress to please myself, no-one else. If you can't handle it, that's your problem," and in defiance would add an extra touch of decadence; perhaps an ankle chain or a nose stud. But suspect what they might, her critics could never prove anything against her.

* * *

The coach driver turned the key to start the engine. After last night, all he wanted to do was to sleep for a week and he'd have thought that most of his passengers would feel the same way. But unluckily for him, they had insisted on continuing with the tour, in search of new experiences. Some idiot in Valhalla had told them about the Native American Heaven, the Happy Hunting Grounds, and how it was the only way to commune with nature and discover the inner self. He drove onwards, following the sketchy map drawn on the back of a beermat and looking for the next turn. At last he reached a slip road forking off to the left: Route 666, the road to Hell.

CHAPTER 3

Julia had decided that she could not allow her bitter disappointment to poison the rest of her afterlife. Already she regretted the wasted years spent longing for the reunion with Martin, years when her only diversion had been her career. She would be damned if she'd carry on in the same way now she was dead; there must be something constructive for her to do.

The tourist information office advised her to start with the Paradise Cultural Complex. This seemed like a good idea, so Julia headed towards it, making first for the museum.

It looked just like any old museum from the outside, a majestic facade with its entrance flanked by pillars. Just inside the entrance there were signs pointing in two directions: "Nostalgia" and "New Experiences". Julia headed towards "Nostalgia", where everything that had ever happened in the history of the world could be experienced or simply observed. She found herself in a representation of her own past, the one place where she had no desire to be. She turned back to the entrance to the "New Experiences" section, where a sign advised her that visitors to the museum could, if they wished, relive their own pasts, or at least the parts that they had enjoyed. Alternatively, if they preferred, they could relive someone else's; Napoleon's, for instance, Cleopatra's, Leonardo da Vinci's, Casanova's – these were all popular – or invent one from scratch. Visitors could even invent new futures.

Next, she visited Paradise Library, which kept every book ever written – and there was no need to search through endless, musty shelves. The Library staff angels knew what everyone wanted and could produce it, instantly – unless, of course, the visitor was one of those curious creatures who actually enjoyed browsing along bookshelves for centuries, in which case they were allowed to search for themselves.

There was an immense reference section, a repository of all the answers to all the questions that anyone could ever ask, the solutions to life's great mysteries, such as "What was the Mona Lisa smiling about?", "Where's Lord Lucan?", and "Where do all the odd socks go?" But it was a reference section with a difference: enquirers didn't always get the true answer, but the answer that would make them happy. Julia bumped into one man who told her that he had spent years trying to prove his theory that history repeated itself again and again; that civilisations advanced up to a point when they destroyed themselves and were then replaced by another society that would, in turn, repeat the pattern. He had been delighted to lay his hands on documentary evidence confirming that Stonehenge was indeed the remains of a multi-storey car park.

The Library also kept a wealth of information on the facilities for education, vocation and amusement available. There were courses in every conceivable subject, Swahili at the Babel School of Languages and harp lessons at St Cecilia's School of Music, to name but two. Julia left the Library with a bundle of leaflets and prospectuses.

Then she visited the Art Gallery, stocked, of course, with every work of art that had been, or would ever be, produced. With all that was on offer Julia couldn't understand why she still felt so despondent. She could even have a job, if that was what she wanted. Every type of employment was possible in Heaven, but it all seemed so artificial and futile. There were an infinite number of factories producing unnecessary goods, shops to sell them and offices to do the paperwork, but it was all an illusion, something to keep workaholics happy. There were even hospitals for people who wanted to play doctors and nurses. Apparently, an angel informed her, they didn't go short of patients, as there were more than enough hypochondriacs to go round. It was obvious to Julia that the only real work was done by the angels. Everything else was merely play-acting, a panacea for boredom.

Julia sighed. This was supposed to be Heaven, but she might just as well be in Hell.

She left the Cultural Complex and headed back towards the hostel. She felt like walking; it would give her a chance to relax and refresh her thoughts, so she willed the journey to take a long time. As she walked, Julia took in her surroundings with a newly-awakened eye. On first glance, Heaven looked pretty much like Earth; roads, buildings, trees, hills. But when she looked closer, the ordinary objects took on a magical aspect. Buildings, apparently constructed of bricks and mortar, concrete or stone, were found, on close examination, to comprise a myriad tiny precious stones arranged in exquisite patterns. As Julia contemplated the pavement, marvelling at the fact that the sparkle she had thought was due to frost, was actually caused by millions of diamonds, she noticed a young angel sweeping the road. Julia recognised her as the angel who had welcomed her into Heaven. "Hello again," she said.

The angel's eyes widened and her hand flew up to her mouth as she stepped back. "It's you! Oh dear, I am sorry. Oh, I'm not supposed to talk to humans."

"There's no need to be frightened," said Julia, putting her hand on the angel's shoulder. "Why should you be sorry, and why aren't you allowed to talk to me?"

"Because it's my fault – your unhappiness." Faced with the victim of her mistake, the Angel Tracey was in some distress. "I should have told you about your husband, but I didn't notice until it was too late. Now they say that I'm a liability, that I don't present the right image."

"Don't worry," said Julia, "I don't blame you, anyone can make a mistake." She paused, looking thoughtfully at Tracey. "Did you lose your job because of that?"

Tracey nodded and looked down at her sweeping brush.

"But that's terrible. They didn't tell me at your office they were going to do this. I would never have let them sack you on my account, believe me."

Tracey shook her head and muttered, "It wasn't the first time." Then in a rush, it all started to come out; how she tried so hard to do exactly what they told her, but how it always seemed to go wrong. How the other angels laughed at her; most of them had been in Heaven for ever and Tracey had only arrived quite recently.

"Come and sit down," Julia said. She led the weeping angel to a wooden seat that had appeared on the pavement. "Tell me how you came to be an angel."

"Jesus takes the little babies who have died after baptism and makes them into angels," Tracey said, reciting the words as if she had learnt them by rote.

"So you came to Heaven when you were a baby and grew up here?"

Tracey looked puzzled. "Grew up?"

"You know, playing with the other little angels and going to school?"

Tracey shook her head, still puzzled. "I did an induction course just before I started work."

Julia frowned. "Did you want to be an angel?"

"It's what I am. It's a wonderful honour to be chosen to be an angel." Again, it was obvious that Tracey was repeating words that she had been taught.

"How cruel," said Julia, "and this is supposed to be Heaven. Tracey, listen to me. Your childhood has been stolen from you. I don't suppose you've ever had the opportunity to make friends, to play with toys – to be in love?" Tracey's blank look confirmed her suspicions and she put her arms round her. "Well you've got as much right as anybody to lead a normal life, and I'm going to do everything I can to help you."

* * *

Martin crept back into the house, hoping that Lucy hadn't missed him. He was unlucky; Lucy had realised the moment he had left, and was now waiting, arms folded, in the hallway.

"Where do you think you've been?" she demanded.

"Just for a walk." He smiled sweetly.

"Don't lie to me, Martin Davis. I can tell when you're lying. You've been to see her, haven't you?" The way her narrowed eyes bored into his reminded Martin of the way Julia had looked at him.

"But I had to see her, it's only fair. I needed to explain." It sounded weak.

"So why didn't you tell me where you were going, instead of sneaking out like a thief in the night?"

"I knew how you'd react, that's why," he said, defensively. "I knew you'd be angry."

"But not as angry as I am now."

"I'll go up to my room until you calm down." He made a move but Lucy barred his way.

"You haven't got a room anymore." Her eyes were glinting. "But you'll find a nice new potting shed out in the garden."

"That's not fair." But Martin knew that he was wasting his breath and he slunk out of the back door. He wondered what he'd ever done to deserve this; one moment he had one wife, the next two, and the next, neither was speaking to him. Martin didn't understand why they were so angry; it wasn't as if he'd deliberately set out to deceive or to hurt anybody, he was just a victim of circumstances. Well, for the time being, he would just have to keep out of their way; he'd had about enough of nagging women recently. Perhaps

46

some time on his own to think was just what he needed.

As Martin wandered down the path to his new temporary home, he noticed a glow escaping from the window of the shed and comforted himself that at least Lucy had provided him with some light. He opened the door of the shed and saw the figure of a woman lying on a bed of feathers, dressed all in white. It was Julia, no, it was Lucy, then Martin realised that the feathers were wings.

"I'm Gloria," said the figure, "I'm your Guardian Angel and I'm really pissed off." She glared at him with narrowed eyes, looking uncannily like both of Martin's wives.

"Good God, what am I supposed to have done to you?" he asked.

"Well usually a Guardian Angel's responsibilities come to an end when her charge enters the afterlife." Gloria lit a cigarette with trembling hands. "Then she, or he, can look forward to a nice long spell of recuperation in the Heavenly Convalescent Home, until the next client comes along. I needed that rest, Martin – I had to undergo intensive group therapy after you died."

"I don't understand."

"No, you wouldn't. That's because I did my job so well, but it wasn't easy. Even as a little baby you were more trouble than you were worth. I've lost count of the number of times I had to pull your inquisitive little fingers away from plug sockets and pans of boiling water." She took a long pull on her cigarette. "Then, as soon as you could walk, you seemed to develop some attraction to busy roads, open windows in high buildings and dangerous dogs." She shook her head. "You don't realise how many near misses you've had. I hate to say this, Martin, but it was almost a relief when that truck flattened you. By that time I was practically burnt-out."

"I'm sorry, but it's hardly my fault that I was accident-prone. Anyway, that doesn't explain why you're here now."

"Isn't it obvious? You're in trouble, Martin. Ever since Julia turned up, you've been lying, deceiving your wives – now that's the sort of thing that could get you thrown out. So I've been sent to get you back on the straight and narrow – keep a close eye, make sure that you're not tempted into more mischief."

"So you'll be following me?"

"Every step of the way, sunshine, and don't think I'm happy about it either." She stubbed out her cigarette in a plant pot. "Now I'm going to get some shut-eye. You'll have to sleep on the floor. And don't get any fancy ideas about sneaking off, I've got eyes in the back of my head and I'll be watching every move you make." The Angel Gloria yawned, stretched her long, white limbs and shut her eyes.

* * *

"If you'd like to take a look at the screen or, if you prefer, figure 1a on page 2 of the report, I'll explain the concept," began Hiram.

Paul looked at Peter and pulled a face. They were sitting in Hiram's latest creation, a conference room equipped with the most sophisticated audio-visual presentation aids: TV and video, overhead projector, slide projector, hologram projector, screen, flip-chart, lecture style seating, perpetual coffee machine. They each had their own copy of the report: a full-colour glossy packed with statistics and computer-generated images. As well as the Trustees, all the Departmental Directors were present: St James (Housing); St Martha (Information), St Thomas (Planning) and St Andrew (Education and Leisure). Hiram stood at the front.

"What I propose," he continued, "is a three-pronged approach to promote and revitalise Heaven, to remind people on Earth what Heaven is like while, at the same time, finding out what they expect and making sure that we can fulfil those expectations." He switched on the overhead projector and a list of words appeared on the screen: "MARKET RESEARCH RATIONALISATION PROMOTION"

"Let's take the first stage," he said, "Market Research. Now until we know what people want, there's no point in rationalising Heaven."

"But we've already been reorganised beyond all recognition," complained Paul.

"Believe me, I've only skimmed the surface – " said Hiram, shaking his head, " – put in place the basic structure to enable us to go on to the next stage. It's likely that we're gonna have to make many more drastic changes before we're finished."

"Over my dead body," muttered Paul under his breath.

Hiram clicked a button on his remote control and, as the image on the screen changed, the screen itself expanded to an infinite size. "Now, gentlemen, here we have a graph showing the improvement in the standard of living on Earth over the past two thousand years. You'll find the same graph on page 5 of your report if you want to study it later.

"What I'm trying to get at," he continued, "is that people are used to better things now, so Heaven's gotta be able to outclass life on Earth in every conceivable way."

"But, with respect, it does," Peter interrupted. "Our citizens can create their own personal Heaven."

"Exactly," said Hiram. "So what we end up with is a free-for-all, where everyone does their own thing, which involves a massive duplication of effort and a waste of people's energy. That's just the sort of thing I've been trying to discourage. We should be taking the lead, presenting our citizens with a range of ready-made packages on a themed basis."

Paul laughed. "Don't tell me, Heaven as a theme park. Disneyland perhaps?"

"Why not, if that's what the punters want. We gotta make them want to come here so bad they'll do anything, even say their prayers and go to church on Sundays. But we're jumping the gun, we can't make any firm decisions until we've completed our research." He pressed a button and the image changed to reveal a world map, covered with coloured dots. "Our targets, gentlemen."

The Saints sat back in their seats, mourning the loss of sanity to their establishment.

Hiram was undeterred. "The only way to find out what people want is to ask them, so I propose to conduct an opinion poll on a sample of the population."

"Are you talking about actually going down to Earth?"

"Sure – why not? Most of the survey work will be carried out by a team of angels, but I was planning on making a few personal visits. In fact, it might be a good thing if we all went down and took a look. I suppose you could describe it as a field trip, a fact-finding mission."

"You can't do that," said Peter. "Visitations are only permitted on very rare occasions – emergencies. Interface with mortals has to be handled very sensitively."

"I know," said Hiram, "I was a mortal, remember? And not too long ago, unlike the rest of you, I might add. Besides, this is an emergency."

"Well you'd have to have the proper authorisation," said Peter. "And that's something the Trust isn't empowered to give you."

"So what are you saying, I gotta ask God, right? Well that's hunky dory with me. To tell you the truth, I'm kinda looking forward to a pow-wow with the Almighty. Look, I can understand you being cautious, but you brought me in to do a job and I can hardly do it with my hands tied behind my back, can I?" He paused and looked each of the others in the face. "Well, what's it to be, guys, am I wasting my time?"

"Let's hear what he's got to say," said Luke. "I'm interested in Hiram's ideas and I'm sure God would be willing to consider the plan if it's a good one."

"That's my boy," said Hiram. "I don't wanna hear people telling me what I can't do, I want 'em to tell me how I can. Now, do I carry on with my presentation?"

The saints looked at each other.

* * *

They tumbled, laughing, out of the main gates, bedecked with streamers, wearing party hats and clutching carrier bags, full of infernal souvenirs, along with their cameras. Two tuxedo-clad demons, built like brickhouses, stood at the gates, arms folded and faces grim.

"And don't come back!" one of the demons cried, unfolding his arms and jabbing a scaly finger towards the revellers. "We don't want your sort in here."

The Japanese, still laughing, turned to wave goodbye. Fifty-two flash guns popped in unison as the moment was captured for posterity. Then they piled back on to the coach and began emptying the carrier bags to admire their souvenirs. The driver shook his head, switched on the engine and manoeuvred the coach out of the car park. Approaching the junction of Route 666 and the Highway to Heaven, he spotted a road to the left, signposted "Earth".

"Oh well," he muttered, flicking the left indicator lever, "worth a try."

* * *

"You'd better wait here while I speak to Him, see what sort of mood He's in," said Peter. He stood with Hiram at the edge of a desert on a small, uninhabited planet in the galaxy of Andromeda. Uninhabited, that was, except for one Deity.

"If you're sure," shrugged Hiram, "I guess you know the guy." His casual attitude hid his true thoughts, for this was a moment he had dreamt of all his life, and now his afterlife: the opportunity to meet the ultimate hero, the big J.C. Although he knew that God was a trinity of Father, Son and Holy Ghost, three in one, Hiram always liked to picture Him in the Jesus mode, representing the down-to-earth characteristics he most admired. He had therefore been pleased to hear that this was how God tended to appear to His subjects. However, instead of the elation he had expected, Hiram felt nervous, lacking in confidence, knowing that God could see all his little faults and weaknesses. There was no bullshitting the big J.C., no matter how much Hiram could talk the halo off a saint or the wings off an angel.

Peter left Hiram kicking his feet around in the sand, and set off to look for God. He found Him crouched on the ground some way off, drawing pictures in the sand with a stick.

"Hello," said God. "I wondered how long it would be before one of you turned up. I suppose it was too much to ask for a bit of peace for a few centuries."

"I'm sorry, Lord," said Peter, "But we're in a bit of a mess over in Heaven. It's this Hiram chap . . ." He was about to tell God all about it, but then realised that God must know already.

"I suppose it's my fault," God said sadly. "I've mollycoddled you lot for too long, I should have delegated more. I thought that it wasn't too late, that if I left you alone for a while, you would all find your inner strengths, your independence. But what do you do? You just go and find yourself another boss." He carried on tracing designs in the sand.

"I'm sorry," said Peter.

"Stop saying you're sorry. I made you, didn't I? It seems I cocked up the design, that's all. I'll do better next time."

"Anyway, I've brought Hiram over. It seems the others think he's got some plans worth considering."

"Yes, yes," said God. "Go on then. Fetch this Yank of yours."

Peter returned moments later, with Hiram grinning nervously

by his side. God looked up at him and smiled in a mysterious way before looking down again at His sand pictures.

"Leave us alone, Peter," He said, and Peter left. "I like deserts," said God, "I always do my best thinking in deserts. They're very peaceful – usually."

"I'm mighty sorry to disturb you, Sir," said Hiram.

God waved the apology away. "I've had all that apology stuff from Peter. Come here and sit down. What do you think?" He pointed at the sand drawings. Hiram squatted beside Him and looked down. Some of the stick figures were based on the human form, but with variations; different shapes and numbers of heads and bodies. Then there were creatures with four legs, a long tail curled at the end like a shepherd's crook, pointed ears and whiskers.

"Foxes?" enquired Hiram.

God frowned. "Oh dear, is that what they look like? They're supposed to be cats. I thought they were rather good, myself. Still, drawing was never my forte. I was thinking of making Felix the dominant race next time, what do you think?"

"Whadaya mean?" Hiram was alarmed. "You're gonna let cats take over the Earth?"

"Oh no, that would never do. Earth's already enough of a mess without introducing species warfare. I'm going to start afresh." God drew a circle in the sand.

"You mean here?"

"No, somewhere far away, where there can be no possibility of interplanetary warfare. I know what those buggers on Earth are like."

"But why cats?"

"I like cats. They're straightforward; they know exactly what they want from life: food, lots of sleep and the occasional bonk. I doubt they'll give me half as much trouble." He stopped drawing and gazed gloomily into the distance. "But I suppose it'll turn out like it did before. After all, the apes were all right until they started evolving."

"It sounds like you've given up on the human race," said Hiram.

"Oh no. They've given up on me. They've got too sophisticated, too self-sufficient, they've got no time for me anymore. I don't know where I went wrong with them."

"Gee, Sir, you can't blame yourself for Man's mistakes."

"Can't I?" said God. "It was me that gave them free will, after all. But then, without it, their worship would have been meaningless."

"So what you gonna do now? Scrap the Earth and start a new cat planet?"

"I wasn't thinking of doing anything about Earth, they're quite capable of bringing about Armageddon by themselves. But I would like to try again, perhaps with cats, perhaps with another species. I could even start off a whole series of experiments, each with a different dominant species." God drew something that looked like a frog.

"That brings me round to what I wanted to talk to you about," said Hiram, "a chance to bring Mankind back into the fold. They're not all bad, you know."

"If you want to have a go, that's fine by me." God shrugged His shoulders. "It's not as if I had any special plans for them."

"I'll need a little more than just your approval."

"Oh?" God raised an eyebrow.

"Well . . ." Hiram began nervously, "I kinda need you to make one or two personal appearances on Earth."

"I don't know about that," said God, picking up His stick again.

"It'd sure be a big help," said Hiram, "I'll tell you what, I'll help you out with your project – you know, trying out new species and all that – on a sort of free trial basis with no obligation and, if you like what you see, then we'll negotiate. Whadaya say?"

"Sounds fair enough," said God. "Come back when you've got something for me." He smiled that mysterious smile again, this time in farewell, although Hiram could have sworn that there was an added element of, dare he even think it, deviousness?

After they had left, God smiled to himself. He wasn't surprised by the way things were going. By leaving the saints in control, He'd effectively given them free will, and He knew by experience what that led to. Freedom brought with it the capacity to make bad decisions as well as good. It had been their choice to appoint Hiram, and they would have to deal with the consequences. Hiram meant well, but he questioned too much, and it had been human curiosity which had led to his species' first big mistake, with the apple.

* * *

Back in Heaven, Hiram found Peter and the others waiting for him.

"Well?" they asked. "Did He say yes?"

"Not exactly." Hiram grinned. "But I'm working on it."

* * *

The fabric of Heaven was woven with imagination and was basically an illusion. Whilst ordinary citizens could create those environments and objects immediately personal to themselves, they were unable to sustain a shared environment beyond the home. For instance, when they went for a walk, they could create roads, paths and beautiful countryside; but the illusion would shimmer away as soon as the creator was out of sight. In fact, there was no real need for Heaven to take on a physical form; it was perfectly possible for souls to float around happily in an abstract Heaven without an imitation of their Earthly existence, but as with the institution of marriage, Heaven was about being happy – and ex-Earthlings were invariably only happy when they were busying themselves in the tedious details of everyday life: shopping and watching endless episodes of their favourite soap operas.

Since the beginning, the task of creating and maintaining this illusory infrastructure had been the angels' responsibility; they had operated as an immense, well-oiled, efficient, yet invisible machine. But Hiram's approach had revolutionised their role, requiring them to maintain a highly visible presence and providing what he liked to describe as a "customer-friendly interface". This created a lot of extra work for the angels – which, the Saints had implied to Hiram, was exactly what made them happy. But the angels weren't happy, they weren't happy at all. It wasn't the actual work they objected to, but the fact that they weren't appreciated: that they weren't consulted. Saints and citizens alike just took them for granted.

"Just listen to this," said the Archangel Gabriel, reading from Hiram's Citizens' Guide at the inaugural meeting of the Democratic Union of Angels and Archangels. "'LITTER AND REFUSE – Don't worry – the angels will take care of it.' Well, ain't that just fine and dandy. Another dirty job, but don't you Heaven-dwellers worry your pretty little heads about it, what are angels for anyway if not to clean up your shit? Do you know, comrades," he leaned forward from the pulpit, brandishing the offending document, "that we actually merit a separate reference in this worthy tome?" He opened it up again and read out loud, "'ANGELS – see under LITTER AND REFUSE, ROADS, PUBLIC BUILDINGS, MAINTENANCE OF' . . . Need I go on? Workhorses, that's all we are to them, and that's all we'll ever be if we don't do something about it."

"He's right," said the Angel Frank, who wore a T-shirt sporting the caption "Angels do it on the wing" and a cartoon of two angels in a compromising position. "Let's see how they get on without us. Things will soon start falling apart."

"It may well come to that, brother, but first things first. I suggest that we draw up a list of demands and submit it to management, and if they don't agree, then we can discuss what action to take. And now, brothers, is a particularly good time for us to take our stand. I have it on very good authority that the saints are planning a major initiative, a publicity campaign directed at Earth, and we all know that they won't get very far without our co-operation."

* * *

"I wish you'd tell me what all this is about," said Peter. He and Hiram were on their way to see God, followed by a procession of angels carrying large cardboard boxes. "I don't like this secrecy, and as Chairman of the Trust – "

"Chairperson," corrected Hiram, who was trying to bring the concept of political correctness into the language of Heaven.

Peter ignored the correction. "As Chairman of the Trust, I think that I have a right to be kept informed."

"All will become clear soon," said Hiram.

"Ooh, this looks intriguing." God fell upon the packages and started to rip them open. "It's just like Christmas."

"Please, Lord," said Hiram, "this is sensitive equipment. Let me set it up for you, it won't take long." He handed God a colourful box. "Would you like to look at this while you're waiting? There's a manual inside."

God looked at the box.

TOOGOOD COMPUTER SOFTWARE presents:
RECREATOR – THE MOST POWERFUL GOD
SIMULATION GAME IN THE UNIVERSE
Create an infinite number of worlds with an infinite
number of species. Select any permutation from an
infinite number of habitats and climates – then watch
your worlds evolve.

'Amazing, out of this world.'

– Celestial Computer Magazine

'Enough in this game to keep you riveted until
Doomsday.' *– Heavenly Megadrive Monthly*

"Hey," said God, "this looks pretty neat."

"I thought you'd like it," said Hiram. "It means you can try out all your ideas without all the time and trouble involved in the real thing. No need to wait millions of years for the results. You can find out which combinations work, then, when you find one you're happy with, do it for real. It's quite easy to play, I'm sure you'll pick it up in no time."

"I should hope so," said God, looking just a little annoyed. "I am all-powerful and all-knowing. Now leave me to play with my new toy. I'll send for you when I'm ready to discuss our deal. In the meantime, I've no objection to you making a start on your market research." He smiled. "But don't forget, no promises about a Second Coming, I haven't made a decision yet."

* * *

The driver pulled off to a services coach park on the M25. The Japanese were still taking everything in their stride, and eagerly enthused on all they had seen on their extended cultural tour of England. The driver was left with the problem of what to do next. He couldn't take them back to where they'd started, he was sure of that. He didn't really understand what was happening to them. One minute, everything seemed solid, the next, the coach would shimmer and disappear only to rematerialise elsewhere. He was pretty certain that they were dead, but he was the only one who seemed to realise this and he didn't want to be the one to break it to the Japanese. Besides, they showed no signs of wanting to go home. The only option left to him was to carry on driving around until someone, anyone, told him otherwise.

He gradually became aware that the level and pitch of background noise had grown, and turned round to find his passengers in a state of considerable agitation. Their souvenirs from Hell, the belts, shoes and handbags that they'd brought from that renowned accessory shop, "Hell For Leather", were disintegrating around them into pools of foul-smelling slime.

CHAPTER 4

Wild Wally was the King of the Road, the convoy of bikers his loyal subjects, and today was the perfect day for a burn-up on the motorway: dry, with a bright, cloudless sky.

The thick wall of fog agreed that it was a perfect day. It wedged itself firmly across all six lanes of the M1, soaking up the warm sun and laughing at the astonished looks on the faces of the bikers as they hurtled towards it.

The bikers slowed down as they penetrated the fog, which wrapped itself mischievously around them. They could see no further than a few feet in any direction, just enough for each to see the biker immediately in front or at the side. Wild Wally, at the apex of the convoy, saw nothing but fog. He had only his instinctive sense of direction to pilot him and his gang through the murk. Suddenly he spotted an executive coach a few feet ahead of him. He focused on the rear lights of the coach and followed it as it veered to the left, onto a nice, new, but unfortunately unfinished motorway bridge.

Wild Wally's last conscious thought as he and his faithful followers plummeted towards the ground, was "Where the fuck did that coach disappear to?"

* * *

As Julia walked towards Eternity Hall, the celestial civic offices, she took in the hubbub of street afterlife. A proliferation of people had gathered together, to talk, to laugh, and to browse among the many stalls. Some were selling food and drink, others clothes, books. A number were selling souvenirs, including wooden spice racks made from the "original cross" and little ornaments made from the "one and only Ten Commandments". One of the most popular fast food outlets was the Loaves and Fishes Sandwich Bar, with its house speciality, fishpaste sandwiches. From time to time the joint proprietor, Saint Honorius, would turn to his partner, Saint Michael, and ask, "How many loaves and fishes have we got left?", to which Michael would reply, "Five and three." "That's plenty then," Honorius would say, with a chuckle. Another stall sold bottles of the celebrated Vin de Cana.

Outside the main entrance to the civic offices, stood the same group of people who had greeted Julia so enthusiastically on her arrival. With their drawing pads and pencils, they hastily sketched or photographed new arrivals. Each was dressed in bright, if somewhat mismatched, clothes. One of them, a young man, smiled at Julia. It was the sort of smile that men had given her when she was thirty, forty years younger and she felt herself blush. What was he looking at her like that for, she wondered; then as she self-consciously put her hand up to her face, she remembered all the years she'd shed.

In return she cast her eye over his appearance, but found it a little too avant garde for her conservative taste: a sort of crinoline meets kimono meets punk. He showed his latest sketch to Julia and explained that he and the others were capturing the fashions as they arrived in Heaven.

"You haven't been here long, have you?" he said.

"Is it that obvious?"

"Don't worry, we all had that lost soul look when we first arrived, you'll soon settle in. My name's Jeff, by the way." He held out his hand for Julia to shake.

"Julia. Tell me, how long have you been doing this?" She waved

61

at his drawing pad. "You're very good, you know."

"Quite a while now. It's one of the beauties of Heaven – an inexhaustible supply of time to do what you want in. Before this I was a nuclear physicist, and before that I read all the works of the great philosophers, listened to every piece of music ever recorded and learned the Encyclopaedia Britannica off by heart." He smiled at her. "By the way, that's another reason why I could tell you were new here: you were rushing. There's really no need. Anyway, perhaps I'll see you round again?" He turned back to join the others, who had flocked to a batch of new arrivals.

Julia walked into the building and found her way once again to the Department of Information, this time at the General Inquiries desk. "She approached the angel behind the desk.

"Hello, can I help you?" asked the angel, who was identified by her namebadge as Lisa.

"Yes, please. I'd like to see someone in charge. I want to make a complaint."

The Angel Lisa looked concerned. "Can you tell me what it's about?"

"I don't really want to have to explain it all to you and then go over it all again with someone else," said Julia, who had experienced this before. "Besides, it's about a lot of things."

The angel smiled again, "I just need an idea, so I know which department to send you to."

"OK." Julia sighed. "It's partly to do with an angel who used to work here, name of Tracey; and it's partly about me: what I'm supposed to do for the rest of my afterlife. More specifically, I want to find out about getting a job."

The Angel Lisa nodded, reassuringly. "That's no problem. What would you like to do? You can be anything you want up here, you know."

"Yes I know about that, but you misunderstand me. I've heard all about the make-believe offices and factories, the play-hospitals.

I want to do a real job, something that's actually needed."

The angel looked bemused. "But you don't need to work anymore, that's what we're here for. You're free to enjoy yourself, do what makes you happy. Have you been to the library yet, the books there are . . ."

"No," said Julia, firmly. "To have a proper job, to make a real contribution – that's what would make me happy. In fact, it's the only thing that would make me happy, and I demand it, as my right."

"Oh," said the angel, slightly flustered, "I'd better ask my supervisor." Julia sighed again: she had known this would happen. "Please take a seat, would you like a coffee?"

Julia declined. Food had never been an important part of her life and it hadn't occurred to her to eat or drink anything while she'd been in Heaven. She'd read the section in the Citizen's Guide on the subject: food was optional, as was the performance of all bodily functions.

As she waited, Julia examined some of the posters and notices on the wall of the reception area. They were publicising various societies: The Stoics' Society (Regular meetings, come Hell or high water), The Martyrs' Support Group, The Amnesia Club (Don't forget the next meeting) and countless others. A couple of the bulletins particularly caught her interest:

THE ELVIS PRESLEY FAN CLUB
Latest reported sightings
Is the King on Venus?
The search goes on

and:

THE RED INDIAN CLUB
Reach Across The Stars

Julia heard a commotion behind her and turned to see a group of about forty leather-clad bikers roaring through the Arrivals Lounge on their Harley-Davidsons.

"I'm suing the arse off somebody about this," yelled the leader, a grizzled and hairy mountain of a man. "Someone's going to have to pay, there's a fucking scratch on my engine." Julia watched, spellbound, as they rode out of the entrance shouting, "Scatter, you fairies" at the waiting fashion students.

* * *

The Angel Lisa had gone to see the Angel Heather, who in turn had approached the Angel Darren, the Section Head, who had asked the Angel Samantha, the Divisional Head, who had referred the problem to Saint George, the Deputy Director. Eventually the problem had landed on Martha's desk.

"Oh dear, what am I supposed to do about this?" she asked Maggie, who had slipped away from the Housing Department for a cigarette and a cup of coffee.

"Really, Martha," said Maggie, "it's quite simple, isn't it – just give the poor woman what she wants. You do owe her something, remember, after that cock-up one of your angels made."

"But she wants a real job."

"So?"

"So, only angels do real jobs."

Maggie sighed, tossed her hair and picked up the telephone. "Could you show Julia Davis to the Director's office, please."

"What did you do that for?" Martha lit a cigarette in her panic, forgetting that she didn't smoke, "I don't know what to say to her."

"I suppose you'll leave it to me as usual," hissed Maggie, as Julia was shown into the office.

Martha drew herself up in her chair and tried to look important.

"Please take a seat, Julia, my name's Martha, I'm Director of Information. I understand you've already met my sister, Mary Magdalene."

"Yes, hello again."

"Are you settling in all right?" asked Maggie.

"Well no, not really. I mean, Heaven is a wonderful place to be and all that, but it's not . . . well, it's not as perfect as I imagined it."

Maggie glanced at Martha. They had had a number of such complaints recently.

"Yes, well, I'm sure we can iron out some of those wrinkles for you," said Maggie. "Now I presume you want to make a complaint about the Angel Tracey? Did you not receive a full apology?" She looked at Martha, who nodded anxiously.

"Yes, from both myself and the Archangel Raphael," said Martha. "And the offending angel has been moved to other duties."

"Offending? She's little more than a baby. She's obviously had next to no training for the job, and, from what I understand, no life to speak of. I don't hold her to blame, and she shouldn't have been punished." Julia's face flushed with indignation. "I must say, I'm alarmed at your recruitment methods. Can it really be the case that babies are transformed into angels and are given no free choice in the matter?"

"I hear what you're saying, Julia," said Maggie, smoothly, "but unfortunately we have little influence on the matter. It was Saint Paul's idea to give the babies angelhood. I'm sure he thought he was doing the right thing." She shrugged her shoulders. "But what can I say? He's a man. The most we can do is to get you an interview with him. You're a citizen of Heaven, he's obliged to give you an audience. Perhaps you can get through where we have failed."

"Yes, I'd like to try. I doubt whether Tracey would want her old job back, after what happened, but surely there must be some way for me to help her."

"I'm so glad we've managed to sort things out," said Martha, a smile of relief spreading over her face as she stood up and held out her hand to shake Julia's.

Maggie and Julia both looked at her. "Well, not quite," said Julia.

"The job?" reminded Maggie.

"Oh, that," said Martha, sitting down again. The chair sighed.

"Yes," said Julia, "I feel at a loose end, like I have no purpose, and I want to do something about it."

"Quite understandable," said Maggie, "and you're sure that you don't want to do any of the pseudo-work we offer up here?" She raised an eyebrow. "They say it feels just like the real thing."

"No," said Julia. "I don't want occupational therapy, I want a vocation."

"I'm sorry," said Martha, "it's impossible, I . . ."

"No," said Maggie, "what my sister means is that it is an unusual request, but I'm sure it's not impossible."

"But what would the other saints say, and more to the point, the angels?" said Martha.

"Bugger them. Besides, there'll be plenty of extra work soon, with this new project."

"Maggie, that's supposed to be hush-hush for the moment." Martha looked shocked.

"Is it? I don't remember you saying that it was secret." Her eyes were round with feigned innocence. "Why, I've already told Gabriel all about it."

"Then it will be all round Heaven by now."

"Is there a problem?" Julia enquired.

"Nothing to worry about." Maggie smiled. "Now, what sort of job were you thinking of doing?"

"I'm not sure really, I worked in a variety of jobs when I was alive; office work, mainly in public relations, a bit of shop work. I do have a flair for organising things, although I haven't many formal qualifications or technical skills."

"Don't worry about that, we have the most comprehensive educational and training facilities in the Universe, but I'm thinking that your PR experience might be useful. Leave it with me, I'll see what I can do." They all shook hands and Julia thanked them for their help and left.

"Well," said Martha, sitting back in her chair, "I might as well have not been here. You completely took over, as usual."

"Martha, I'll never understand you." Maggie shook her head and sighed in exasperation at her sister.

* * *

As she walked out of the reception area, Julia felt pleased with the way the interview had gone. She knew her ambitions were modest; she'd never been the crusading type, never wanted to heal the sick, or save the world. She just wanted to have a go at what she was good at, organising things efficiently. It was the kind of work she'd done all her life, but never so single-mindedly as she was prepared to do now.

She carried on past the fashion students, noticing with amusement that many of them were now bedecked in black leathers and chains.

* * *

"I'm afraid you're going to be angry with me," whispered a husky voice into Hiram's ear.

"What?" said Hiram, who was enjoying a mint julep in the new American bar of The Wing and a Prayer, as he struggled to remember the name of that pretty little wife he'd left back on Earth: Patty, Terry, Mamie? He turned to see Mary Magdalene, in a dress so tight he completely forgot his wife in an instant.

"I've been very naughty," purred Maggie, "but I didn't mean it."

"Let me get you a drink, my dear lady, and you can tell me all about it. What'll you have?"

"I'll have what you're drinking. Shall we sit down?"

Hiram followed Maggie to a cosy booth. "What did you wanna tell me?"

"Oh, I hope you won't be cross, it's just that I got to hear about your project and I was so excited about the idea that I've been telling some of my friends." She cast her eyes down and then looked back up at Hiram from beneath her long lashes. "I'm sorry, I didn't know it was supposed to be a secret."

"Hey, no problem," said Hiram. "It was only supposed to be kept quiet until I got the official go-ahead, and now I've got that, you can tell the world."

"Oh, I am relieved." Maggie crossed her legs, letting her skirt hitch up just a few more inches. "I would have been mortified if I'd spoilt things, and all I wanted to do was help."

"Well, young lady," said Hiram, patting her knee, "I sure could use someone like you on the public relations side, I've always reckoned that it needs a feminine touch."

"I'm glad you think so, Hiram, because I've got a friend who's an expert in that field. She might be useful to you. The only trouble is," she pouted her lips, "I don't think the others will allow it. You see, she's not a saint."

"I don't see why that should matter, if she's the right woman for the job." Hiram felt that the saints looked down on him and his "honorary" sainthood and was automatically sympathetic to anyone who suffered from similar prejudice.

"I'm sure she is, Hiram, and what's more, she's a recent arrival, so she knows what's going on down on Earth. Can I bring her to see you?"

"Yeah, bring her along, whenever. Now, how about another drink?"

"I'd love another, Hiram," she smiled, "but unfortunately, I have to get back to work. You know what they say, no peace for the wicked." And with a swing of her hips and after blowing Hiram a kiss, she walked out of the bar.

* * *

In a dark, lonely corner of the crowded bar of The Gate and Trumpet, Martin sat, gazing moodily into his pint. The Angel Gloria was on her eleventh super-strength lager, which seemed, to Martin's dismay, to have made her even more talkative. She was recounting, in an embarrassingly loud voice, stories about Martin's childhood; how he used to cry if his mother went out, how sweet he used to look in his cub scout uniform, how often he used to wet the bed. They were stories that even Martin's mother would have hesitated before telling.

"Oh, Martin," she chuckled, "remember your friend Johnny?"

"No," snapped Martin.

"You must, you know, little Johnny, your imaginary friend? You used to chatter away to him and play pirates in the garden and, oh yes," she threw her head back in hysterics, "remember the time you were deep in conversation with him and you looked up to see the two little girls from next door were watching you as if you were mad, and you ran into the house, crying?"

"No, I don't. You're making all this up. And I've had just about enough of it. I'm going home."

He stormed out of the pub, with Gloria still chuckling and tugging at his arm to remind him of this and that. As Martin headed back to his unwelcoming home, he wondered if there was anywhere on Heaven where he might find a bit of peace and quiet, away from these troublesome women.

* * *

One moment Hiram was sipping his third mint julep in the Wing and a Prayer, the next he was standing next to God in the desert. Fortunately he was still holding his drink.

"I'm sorry to whisk you away from your leisure time," said God, glancing up for a moment before returning His gaze to the computer screen, "but I knew you'd want to hear my decision as soon as possible. Excuse me if I carry on working, but these ants are fascinating."

"Ants?" asked Hiram. "What about the Cats?"

"Oh, progress has been very disappointing. They're just too territorial: Cat World is comprised of millions of tiny nations. You should see the ants though: they're hardworking, community-minded, and you should see their architecture, it's amazing. Look here." He pointed to a crop of pyramids displayed on the screen. "As you can see, they're going through an Egyptian phase at the moment. I'm sorry." He looked up at Hiram again. "I'm afraid I'm getting a bit carried away, but as you've no doubt gathered, I'm pleased with this software, very pleased. So here's my offer: I'll guarantee to make at least one appearance on Earth, the time and venue to be of my choosing. You'll be given advance notice to enable you to publicise the event."

"Only one appearance?" asked Hiram.

"I said at least one, there may be more, but only if I decide that it's appropriate. Is that agreed?"

"It's a deal," said Hiram, and almost before he had finished speaking he found himself back in the bar. God sure wasn't one for small talk.

* * *

Back on Andromeda, God sighed as He examined the screen. He hadn't told Hiram everything. He had watched the worlds develop, but, although their evolution had been artificially accelerated, the

70

various species remained entrapped by their animal natures and this was leading to stagnation. There had been one disk out of those that had come with the software that He'd held back until now, the one labelled "Free Will", hoping that He wouldn't need it. Sighing, He installed the program and watched as it took effect. The Ants' architecture became more innovative, their civil engineering more sophisticated, but as the Ants were free to use their own initiative, they began to cut corners, using shoddy materials and rushing to get the work done faster, just to increase the profit margin. Free will brought the potential for genius and creativity, but it had its price. The disk had been infected with the Satan virus – and would gradually spread evil throughout His simulated worlds.

* * *

In Valhalla, the Hall of Heroes, the Viking Heaven, sat Eggnog the Magnificent. "Bring me another tankard of ale," he demanded of the serving wench. "And don't forget the cherry and the paper umbrella!"

It was Happy Hour, but Eggnog was far from happy. Valhalla had been taken over by a fierce tribe of warriors, clad in armour of leather and chains, with horned helmets. They had rode into Valhalla on fearsome iron, headless horses, which roared and trailed clouds of fire and smoke. The invaders had commandeered the best seats in the house, including Eggnog's regular table next to the great fire, seized the fairest wenches, devoured the juiciest joints of roast boar and quaffed the strongest ale.

Where were the heroes, the fearless Vikings who would fight to the death to repel these invaders? Softened, every last one of them, by centuries of dissipation, they had surrendered to the weakening influence of women and now cared only for the pleasures of the flesh. Eggnog shook his head sadly. The old Eggnog would have thrust himself into battle, inspiring the rest to join him – death before dishonour. But up here there was no death, and without the risk of death, what was there for a brave warrior to fight for?

In the old days, you couldn't just walk into Valhalla, march up to the bar and order yourself a drink. Time was when you had to prove yourself in battle and die a brave and bloody death before you could cross the sacred threshold. But it seemed that even Odin himself had gone soft and now anyone could enter the mighty portals. Just look at that other lot over there, for example, the barbarians from the Orient, with their slanted eyes hidden behind little masks of glass. They were no warriors, for all their shouting in harsh tongues and waving about of black boxes that shot forward bright, dazzling lights. Then there was one amongst them who did not belong, although he drank with them. A member of the race that had been, in Eggnog's time, a sworn enemy of the Norsemen, a Briton. Eggnog could have wept with the shame of it. But the bikers were the main focus of Eggnog's resentment.

If Wild Wally was aware that he was being watched with such hatred, he showed no sign of it. He just sat sprawled on one of the wooden benches with his feet on the table and tankard in his hand. He surveyed his fellow customers with disgust, and spat, with deadly accuracy, into the ashtray on the table. Who the Hell were all these old-timers with their long, matted grey hair and their weird pointy helmets? Wild Wally guzzled the dregs of his pint and grunted in the direction of the nearest serving wench. He would have to see his lawyer about those helmets, obviously a breach of copyright. But first he would have to have a word with the manager of this place – what was his name, Odin? – about getting a jukebox with some decent music on; the Stones, Steppenwolf, Black Sabbath. All those battle anthems and drinking songs were starting to get on his nerves.

* * *

"Come in, sit down, make yourself comfortable," said Hiram, after shaking Julia's hand. He looked at her, appraising her appearance. She was attractive, but not the sort of woman to drive a man to sin, not like Mary Magdalene. She was smartly groomed and wore a grey interview suit. Hiram had made up his mind to employ her before she even opened her mouth to speak; not because of her appearance, but because, like him, she had professed herself willing to do real work in Heaven.

"Maggie tells me you've worked in public relations," he said.

"Yes, but my work was mainly administrative, managing the office, that sort of thing. Others had the ideas, I did the background work." She was honest, Hiram liked that.

"That's what I need," he said, "someone to act as my assistant, keep my papers in order, someone who'll listen sympathetically when I've had enough of those pesky saints. Could you do that?"

"I should think so," she said, smiling.

"Great, you're hired. When can you start?"

"Well I'd like to start straight away, if I may. You can't imagine what this job means to me."

"Right," said Hiram. "Let's start by seeing if there's anyone else up here who wants to get off their butts and get back to work. I need to set up a legal department. Could you arrange for the jobs to be advertised? I've drawn up the job descriptions."

Hiram didn't know what to do with the writ that had landed on his desk. The rumour he'd heard on Earth that Hell's Angels had a tendency to resort to litigation to solve their problems seemed to be well-founded. Not only had they sued Heaven for damage caused to their persons and property on their deaths, but they were claiming copyright on the name "Angel".

* * *

"Have you seen this?" St John was waving a copy of the latest issue of *The Herald* and stabbing with his finger at a full-page advert.

"What's he playing at now?" said Paul. "We haven't authorised this."

"I know, I've already tackled him about it," said Peter. "But you know what he's like, criticism just rolls off him like water off a duck's back. And now he's gained God's approval to his project, he thinks that he can do exactly what he wants."

"But employing ordinary citizens, surely that's not on?"

"That's what I said, but he challenged me to show him the regulations that said he couldn't, and besides, we did set a precedent by employing him in the first place." Peter shrugged his shoulders. "No, we made our own bed and now we've got to lie on it. As I've said before, we can only hope that Hiram will be his own worst enemy, that eventually he'll overstep the mark and incur God's wrath."

* * *

The row of coaches stretched out further than the eye could see: Greyhound Buses, National Express, Tyrolean Post Buses, transport from every nation on Earth, and all of them empty. Hiram frowned as he looked at them, then down at the papers on his clipboard. He checked and double-checked the instructions he'd issued. They'd been perfectly clear; every available angel should have reported for duty by now; those coaches should have been full.

Hearing a sound behind him, Hiram turned. It was the Archangel Gabriel, holding out a scroll.

"On behalf of the Democratic Union of Angels and Archangels," he announced, "I formally submit this list of demands and declare that, until such a time as they are met in full, the angels and archangels are officially on strike." A host of angels marched up to join him, waving placards and chanting, "What do we want? Respect. When do we want it? Now. What do we want? Recognition. When do we want it? Now. What do we want? Responsibility. When do we want it? Now. What do we want? Representation. When do we want it? Now."

"I had no idea that you were unhappy," said Hiram.

"That's probably because you never asked," said Gabriel.

Hiram was sympathetic. "Hey, guys, c'mon. Perhaps I am at fault, but I was assured by the saints that there were no labour relations problems here. It seems that I was misinformed. I promise that I'll give these demands of yours fair consideration, but d'you have to take industrial action? At least give me the chance to sort this out amicably."

"I'm sorry, but we've heard these promises before, from the others. We're officially out and we'll stay out until we get fair play."

Hiram walked back to his office, past the long line of empty coaches, past a group of angels who were wearing donkey jackets and warming their hands on a brazier while singing revolutionary songs, into a building where the structure was already showing signs of decay.

* * *

Saint Paul's eyes narrowed as he watched the woman walk out of his office. Who the Hell did she think she was, telling him how he should do his job? If she was so clever, perhaps she could think of a more efficient and effective way of increasing the angel workforce.

Did she seriously think that people who'd experienced life would be willing to forego the delights of Heaven in return for an afterlifetime of servitude? The old adage rang true, as far as Paul was concerned, you can't miss what you've never had. It made complete sense to use babies, who didn't know any different. Besides, what greater honour could there be than to serve God?

Paul hoped that this would be the last he'd hear of that interfering, officious woman. He was quite pleased with the way he'd managed to fob her off. She'd thought that he was granting her a concession by handing over the responsibility for the Angel Tracey, but as far as Paul was concerned, he was well rid.

* * *

As Hiram walked into his office he was greeted by a thick curtain of black smoke. "What the Hell is going on?"

"It's all right now," Julia coughed and spluttered. "I've managed to put it out."

The air started to clear and Hiram could see that the fire had originated on his desk.

"I'd just put your post in your in-tray," said Julia, "and when I came back in moments later with some photocopying, the blaze was well under way. What do you think it is?"

Hiram examined his in-tray. Among the charred papers, there was a remnant left partially untouched. With a pair of tweezers, he picked it out. It had apparently been a small, white card, edged with black. Hiram could still make out some of the letters printed on it:

SS THEA
ese
ITH THE W
ow A Sea

"Gee," said Hiram, "I guess I won't have the pleasure of seeing Satan perform Miss Scarlett after all."

* * *

Tommy the Tortoise narrowed his eyes as he peered over his neighbour's fence. Why should Terence have the shell with the most striking pattern, the glossiest shine? What had Terence done to deserve the affections of Thelma, the prettiest tortoise in the neighbourhood? Tommy gripped the iron bar tightly. This had gone on too long; after tonight the shell and Thelma would both be his.

The Satan virus moved on.

CHAPTER 5

"What kinda outfit have you guys been running around here?" demanded Hiram, banging his fist on the table. "You gotta major labour relations problem and either you didn't see fit to tell me about it or, even worse, you didn't know it existed." He waved the scroll in the air. "Have you seen this pathetic catalogue of grievances?"

"We don't need to see," said Peter, "we've heard it all before. You're right. It is pathetic. Just rip it up and take no notice."

"When I say pathetic," said Hiram, "I mean that it's pathetic you guys haven't sorted it. You assured me the angels enjoy what they do, now it seems that you've deliberately been ignoring their needs for some time." He waved the scroll again. "I've read their demands and they seem on the level. All they're asking for is the recognition they're entitled to, respect, the chance of promotion and the right to have an input in the decision-making process."

"I really don't think that's a good idea," said Peter. "We've all seen what happens when they get ideas above their station." Paul and John smiled smugly and nodded their agreement.

"Whadaya mean?" asked Hiram.

"Come on," said Paul, "don't tell me you've never heard of the fall of Lucifer?"

"Sure I have," said Hiram. "D'ya mean to tell me that after all this time, you're judging all the angels on the actions of a handful of individuals? Have you forgotten that the angels and archangels here now are the ones who fought against the fallen angels? But I tell you this, if you carry on treating them like shit, I wouldn't be surprised if they do go down to the other side." He looked round at the others. "We're privileged here to have the best workforce at our disposal. That is, if we treat 'em right. I propose to accede to these demands. If you guys insist, we can put it to the vote, but I warn you, if you don't back me on this, I'll take the matter to God for arbitration."

"I don't suppose we've got any choice," muttered Peter.

"I must say I'm impressed," said Paul. "This is a totally new approach to industrial relations. From my limited experience, what usually happens is that both sides start from diametrically opposite positions, with the trade unions asking for a lot more than they could ever hope to achieve and management willing to concede just a little more than they would admit. Then, usually, the two sides move slowly and grudgingly towards middle ground, arrive at an agreement and both claim victory. Yes, Hiram's approach is very novel, no messing about with all those negotiations, just go straight to total, unconditional capitulation. I take my hat off to you, Hiram. I wonder why it has never caught on down on Earth."

* * *

Martha was paying a visit to her friend, Mary, Mother of God (known to her nearest and dearest as Mary Mog), at the headquarters of the Heavenly Helpline. It is not for nothing that little boys and girls are taught to pray to "Our Lady", so that she can intercede with God on their behalf. Until recently the method of dealing with these prayers had been rather informal; Mary Mog had listened, sifted out the more deserving and brought them to God's attention. Hiram had opted for a more professional approach; an office, an assistant, two lines of communication with Earth, and a set of guidelines for responding to prayers.

"Things are getting worse," said Mary. "The number of petitions we're receiving has increased tenfold. See that pile in the corner? Those are just from one organisation, the Society for the Promotion of Rights for the Remarried. And the 'phones are ringing all the time. I desperately need more staff and more telephone lines. The Good Samaritan does his best, but between the two of us we can't cope with this level of problems. Besides, it's getting us both down. You can't imagine how depressing it is listening to people's problems all day, every day. I've even found myself wondering why God doesn't just put the poor little creatures out of their misery."

"It's been bad before, though," Martha said. "I remember what it was like during the Great Wars."

"Well, there's no World War now." Mary took a sip from her tea. "And the worse of it is, for the first time in eternity, we're receiving prayers for help from citizens of Heaven. That shows that something is badly wrong. Ever heard the saying, 'God's in His Heaven; all's right with the World'? Well, God isn't in His Heaven. Draw your own conclusions."

"Have you asked Him to come back?"

Mary shrugged. "Why would He listen to me? I'm only His mother, for God's sake. Anyway, I have tried. I've been to see Him in the desert, but He was so engrossed in one of those new-fangled computer games, that He hardly listened to a word I said."

"The novelty will soon wear off," Martha reassured her. They both sat quietly for a few moments, sipping their tea.

"By the way," said Martha, "I hope you don't mind my asking, but I've seen that lovely spice rack that your Joseph made for Luke. Do you think he could make one for me?"

"I don't see why not. I'll ask him. He's got a lot of work on at the moment, making new bookshelves for the Paradise Library."

"I don't want to bother him if he's too busy."

"He won't mind," said Mary Mog, "he likes to do something different from time to time, to add a bit of variety."

* * *

Ant World had been hit by a terrible tragedy: one of the new pyramids had collapsed on the day of the opening ceremony, killing millions. The insurance company, after a thorough inspection, declared that it was caused by an "Act of God", a term they'd invented specially for the eventuality that anyone might dare to make a claim, and refused to pay out. The inspector's report, which identified a horrifying catalogue of shoddy work, sub-standard materials and deliberate contraventions of health and safety legislation, was hushed up. The Ants were now praying to the vengeful God whose apparent existence they had only recently been made aware of. The skyscraper building programme was put on ice and the architects were busy designing elaborate, towering cathedrals in honour of the new deity.

The Satan virus moved on.

* * *

If Julia was going to take the Angel Tracey under her wing, then she was determined to do things properly. She knew that she couldn't give Tracey the life she'd never had, but at least she could give her a taste of what it was like on Earth. She had decided to start in the Paradise Library. It seemed that Tracey and the other new recruits had, during their artificially accelerated, greenhouse forced, development, learned to read and write, but they had never been taught that these skills could be used for pleasure as well as for work. With the help of the kindly librarian, the Angel Mabel, Julia gathered together a collection of children's classics recommended as suitable educational reading for a young girl.

Leaving Tracey with her pile of books, under the guidance of the Angel Mabel, Julia headed back to the office.

* * *

It was obvious to Hiram that what was needed was a radical rethink, a complete overhaul of the departmental structure. It wasn't just the angels' strike that had prompted this, he'd also received representations from other quarters: Mary Mog, pleading for additional resources for her Helpline; Martha, unhappy in her present job and concerned at the apparent failure of the "Care in the Community" policy, particularly where the Limbo Babies were concerned; Julia, indignant about the angel recruitment scheme. Then there was Maggie, perfumed and seductive, imploring him with thinly-veiled promises in her dark eyes for the chance to head her own department. Hiram decided that the best course of action was to give everybody what they wanted. After all, wasn't that what Heaven was all about?

So he created four new departments: Personnel, with the Archangel Raphael as Director, charged with the task of reviewing angel recruitment; Operational Services, with the Archangel Michael responsible for directing the angels in their everyday work; Communications, headed by the Archangel Gabriel; and Social Services, with Martha in charge, back again doing the one job she loved, looking after the babies. Martha's former job as Director of Information Services was given to a delighted Maggie. Mary Mog was allocated the additional staff and resources she needed.

Everybody would be happy now, Hiram thought.

* * *

"Bloody ridiculous," declared Peter. He was sitting in the bar of the Wing and a Prayer with Paul and John. "What sort of manager gives in to demands just like that? He's a pushover for anyone who comes whining to him." He nodded in the direction of a small but noisy group of Archangels who were celebrating at a nearby table. "Look at that lot over there. Giving them power is like giving a chainsaw to a psychopath."

"Have a drink with us," called Raphael from the other table, "to show there's no hard feelings."

"Piss off, you overgrown budgie," snarled Paul. He turned back to the others. "It's bad enough having to work with that lot without being expected to socialise as well."

Raphael shrugged his wings, laughed and went back to his pint.

* * *

The strike had brought about a blessed respite for Martin. The Angel Gloria, a staunch trade unionist, had not hesitated to take her place at the picket line. Martin had desperately tried to heal the rift with Lucy before his guardian could return, but if anything, she was angrier than before. She'd accused him of having another woman, another "dark-haired hussy", who slept with him in the shed. In vain, Martin tried to explain who Gloria was, but Lucy said she couldn't trust him anymore; she would never believe a word he said, ever again. And then, as if things weren't bad enough, the strike was over and Gloria was back, unbearably smug in her triumph.

"We've even managed to get workforce representation on the Trust, as well as a number of Departmental Directorships," she said. "What's more, now Raphael is Director of Personnel, he'll be drawing up a hierarchical structure for angels, which will mean plenty of opportunities for promotion." She pulled a face at Martin. "I've got my sights set on a nice, cushy desk job, to get me away from you and your miserable face for good."

But Martin wasn't listening. "I've been thinking . . . " he said.

"That explains it," said Gloria. "I thought I could smell burning."

Martin ignored her. "You know all this business about time being flexible? Well, I don't know why I didn't think of it before. All I have to do is to go back in time to when I first arrived in Heaven and tell Lucy about Julia, then go to meet Julia when she arrives and warn her about Lucy. It's so simple."

Gloria yawned. "You're the simple one, Martin. I wish I had a pound for everyone who's come up with that stupid time travelling idea. You've all been watching too much Doctor Who and Red Dwarf. To be blunt, the idea's crap. Sure, you can go back to whatever point in time you want, but you can't alter something that you've already done. In fact, you wouldn't even be able to interact with anybody who knows you. If you went back to any point within your own past, you'd be a paradox, an impossibility, because you would already exist there. You could observe, but not participate. This safeguard is designed to stop the kind of manipulation of time that you've suggested. I'm afraid that the past is now real and fixed in both Julia's and Lucy's memories. Face it, sunshine, your only option is to keep your nose clean until Lucy decides to forgive you, however long that takes."

* * *

The Daily Sphere
MOTORWAY MAYHEM – MULTIPLE MOTORBIKE
CRASH
Police investigating Saturday's M1 crash in which forty motorcyclists were killed are appealing for witnesses to come forward. They are hoping to trace the driver and passengers of an executive coach, which was seen in the vicinity at the time of the accident.

* * *

Mary Mog surveyed her improved headquarters. The shiny push-button telephones represented additional lines of communication with Earth, and each was manned by an angel fully-trained in counselling skills. Every prayer, every petition, would be logged in to the computer and sent, by electronic mail, to the appropriate department.

She sighed. It was all very well, but Hiram had missed the point. When she'd gone to see him about the increasing number of prayers, she had hoped that he'd tackle the root cause of the problem, not just the symptoms. Perhaps she should have come straight out and told him that what was needed was for God to come back and take over, but when it came to the crunch she just didn't want to hurt Hiram's feelings.

* * *

Julia left her office and headed back towards the library, where she found Tracey still sitting at her table, engrossed in a book. In the time that it took Julia to walk from the main entrance to the table, she watched Tracey finish that book, and two others. She joined the Angel Mabel, who was struggling to carry further piles of books over to Tracey's table. Julia picked one up. It was a formula romance, its cover depicting a typical dark, brooding hero and soft, yielding heroine. She picked up some of the other books, all variations on the same theme. Tracey seemed oblivious both to Julia and to the Angel Mabel who was now setting off to find new books to replace those that Tracey had already devoured.

Julia beckoned Mabel back. "Why is she reading this stuff? What about the list you recommended?"

"She went through those like a tornado," said Mabel. "You hadn't been gone long before she started asking for more. She's read all the classics, so I didn't see any harm in giving her the run of the library."

"Well, it wasn't really what I planned, but I suppose it's up to her."

As she spoke, Tracey put down the book she was holding and looked up, her eyes burning with enthusiasm "More?" she pleaded.

"Not now." Julia decided she had to be firm. "You seem to have worked your way through the entire romance section. Mabel's got to get some new stock in for you. I'll take you to the cinema next, to watch some films. At least you won't be able to speed-read those."

But, like every other facility in Heaven, the Paradise Cinema had a unique feature. It was able to project, simultaneously, to each individual, the film that they wanted to see. So, while Julia sat approvingly through The Sound of Music and Mary Poppins, unknown to her, Tracey was watching Doctor Zhivago, Ghost and Gone With The Wind.

* * *

For the second time, Hiram inspected the row of coaches and the queue of angels waiting to board. The Archangel Gabriel was issuing last minute instructions as clipboards, pens, questionnaires and watches were distributed to the angels. "You'll need the watches," Gabriel was saying, "because on Earth, we will be governed by Earth time. You'll be given a set time by which you must return to your coach, and woe betide any angel who's late. You'll be told exactly where to go to collect your information and you must not stray from that point." He spotted a couple of angels giggling. "Yes, and that means you, Kylie and Sophie. No sightseeing, no window shopping, or there will be trouble. Now let's make a start."

Hiram waited until all the angels had boarded the coaches, then stepped on to the one destined for London, England. Now that Hiram had God's word that He would make at least one personal appearance, he wanted to make a start on promoting the event. He had a list of people, mostly respected members of the clergy, pillars of the establishment, who would surely be believed when they announced the Second Coming. Hiram was well aware of the danger that the project could be wrecked by scepticism and, therefore, all publicity had to be handled with the utmost sensitivity.

There was one person on that coach for whom the trip was very special, the Angel Tracey. Hiram had agreed to Julia's request for her to join the survey; she was a pleasant, friendly little thing and Hiram thought she would be good at this type of work. The Archangels had been opposed to the idea and, in the end, had only agreed on the proviso that she be supervised by a more experienced angel.

Julia stood by the roadside, waving them off. Hiram had advised her to take a break while he was away; there would be a lot of work to do after his return, sorting and analysing the results of the survey. She decided to do something she had been putting off ever since she arrived, visit her parents. It wasn't that she didn't love them, but it wasn't all that long ago that they had died, Julia's father two years before her, and her mother only six months. In the final years spent together, the three of them had grown old together in a typically bickering fashion. She'd rationalised her apparent neglect of them since her arrival by telling herself that they wouldn't know she was in Heaven and also, as everyone kept pointing out to her, she had all the time in the world.

* * *

Satan had one main aim, or rather, one all-consuming obsession. Ever since his fall from Heaven following an unsuccessful attempt to overthrow God, he had vowed to return. But he was banned, for eternity, and could only return by invitation or by defeating God, which he knew from sore experience was pretty damn near impossible. Excluded from Heaven, the only place where Satan could do battle was on Earth. It was with great interest, therefore, that he watched the celestial fleet of buses on their journey through the ether to Earth.

"Whadaya gonna do, then, boss?" Mephistopheles skipped playfully round the Devil, twirling his tail. "Put sugar in their engines, let their tyres down?" He laughed inanely. "That'd be a good trick, eh? Like the exploding theatre ticket, that was a laugh, wasn't it, boss?"

"Shut up, you're getting on my nerves," Satan said through gritted fangs. "Make yourself useful, why don't you, and tell Beelzebub I want to see him. I feel like some intelligent conversation for a change."

"Are you sure, boss? Beelzebub's so boring. If you want, we can play hide the sausage again."

"If you don't piss off, you'll be a burnt sausage," Satan hissed, his eyes blazing.

Mephistopheles scuttled away, his tail between his legs, and moments later, Beelzebub arrived.

"You sent for me, Your Satanic Majesty?"

"Yes." Satan glanced over at his most trusted advisor. Mephistopheles was right, Beelzebub was boring, but he was loyal, sensible and he showed respect. "Have you seen those?" He pointed his talons at the procession of coaches.

"Yes, sir. I've been watching them."

"I'd like to find out what they're up to. How do you fancy a little trip to Earth?"

"Whatever you say, Sir. Would you like me to follow the first coach? I think I recognised our American friend sitting at the front."

"You really do have the most remarkable eyesight, Beelzebub. Yes, that would be a good idea. You can use my car. And take a few demons with you, they can check out what the angels are doing while you follow the American." He dismissed the demon with a wave of his hand.

"Yes, Your Lowness. Would you like me to send Mephistopheles back in?"

"No, tell him I've got a headache."

* * *

The procession of coaches drove onward through the ether, diverging as they reached the planet's atmosphere, each heading for a different destination. The targets had been carefully and scientifically selected; a representative sample of cities, towns and villages from every nation on Earth. Each angel had been given a quota of the people they were to approach, categorised by age, gender and occupation, carefully calculated to cover a cross-section of the Earth's population.

Behind the coaches, unseen by the angels, a sleek black limousine, numberplate "EVIL 1", glided silently through space.

Each coach stopped in a car park, or in the case of the less developed countries, in a clearing. The arrival of coachloads of angels attracted little attention in the large cities, and only marginally more in smaller places. Most people gave a cursory glance, then dismissed the whole thing as a publicity stunt or marketing exercise, which was exactly what it was.

The first person to be approached by an angel was Mrs Shirley Watkins of Daventry. Mrs Watkins, struggling with two heavy bags of shopping and one screaming two-year-old, took one look at the Angel Jason, who had just asked her what her idea of Heaven was, and snapped, "If you're trying to sell me a sodding timeshare, you're wasting your time," before marching off towards the bus stop.

This type of reaction, although by no means isolated, was in the minority. Those people who stopped long enough to listen to the angels for more than a few seconds, those who looked into their deep, beautiful eyes, were soon captivated by their spell. They answered the questions with eloquent honesty then, at the end of the interview, went on their way, forgetting the substance of the encounter, but carrying away with them a feeling of peace and lack of fear for the future.

The demon Jake, undercover in jeans and a leather jacket, watched the angels from a distance. There were two that he was particularly interested in. Whilst most of the angels carried out their interviews alone, these two stuck together. It was obvious to Jake that the younger one was an inexperienced trainee. He waited patiently until the older angel allowed her charge to start interviewing on her own, then casually strolled towards her at the very moment when she was looking for someone to talk to.

Tracey looked at the young man and smiled at him. "Would you mind answering a few questions? It won't take long."

"I'm all yours, sweetheart," he said, looking piercingly at her through cold blue eyes, "for as long as you like."

Tracey blushed. None of the people to whom the Angel Heather had spoken had acted like this. They'd just gone into some sort of trance and answered the questions. She looked away from the young man's face and started to read the questions from the survey form.

"Let me have a look," said the young man, pulling Tracey's clipboard towards him. "I tell you what, I'll take one of these away with me, then I'll come back when I've filled it in."

"No, you can't . . ." Tracey began, but the young man had already snatched away one of the forms and disappeared down a side street.

"What's happened now?" asked Heather, who had noticed that Tracey was in distress.

"That man, he's stolen one of my forms."

"Is that all? He was probably just teasing you. Don't worry, the form won't tell him anything. It's just a list of questions, there's nothing to identify where it's come from."

"I'm not so sure." Tracey shivered. "There was something strange about him." But Heather had already moved away and was busy interviewing another member of the public.

Just around the corner, Jake examined his booty. Perhaps this piece of paper would be his passport out of Demon school, if he was clever, and made sure that he got it into the right hands. He wasn't going to let Beelzebub, or any of the other demons, take credit for his work this time.

CHAPTER 6

Beelzebub, fading into the background in grey slacks and an anorak, followed Hiram to the Church of the Saviour. He watched as Hiram shimmered into invisibility before entering the church. Taking a deep breath, Beelzebub followed suit.

It is a common misconception that the Devil and his disciples cannot enter a church or set foot, or cloven hoof, on consecrated ground. True, it was a deeply unpleasant experience and was impossible for most of the lower orders of demons, but it was within the capabilities of an old hand like Beelzebub; and he had been given explicit instructions not to let Hiram out of his sight. He was well aware that the penalty for disobeying Satan's orders was far more painful than the experience he was now preparing to face. So he slipped unseen into the church and took up a post from where he could watch.

Father Gaylord Sorrell was at prayer, his head bent in humility. Hearing the sound of a throat being cleared, he raised his head and beheld the vision that hovered above the altar.

"Hiya." The vision spoke with an American accent. The priest watched in amazement as the spectre descended, solidified, then leant on the side of the altar, smoking a fat cigar.

"Lord?" asked Father Sorrell, with a mixture of awe and incredulity, as he wondered whether one of the altar boys had been putting illegal substances in the communion wine again.

"Well," the vision drawled, "I guess you could say I'm one of His deputies – Saint Hiram, how d'ya do. We like what you've been doing down here, Gaylord. OK if I call you Gaylord? We reckon you've got the kind of approach we need right now." He strolled around the altar, picking up and examining the chalice. "Gold plate? Tut-tut," he muttered. "As I was saying, Gaylord old buddy, we've got an exciting new project in the offing and we could use you to help with some advance publicity. Whadaya say?"

Father Sorrell blinked twice, but the vision remained. And what's more, it was holding out something in its hand, a scroll of some sort. The priest reached out, his hands trembling, and took the scroll from Hiram. Perhaps, he thought, it was a message from God, a new set of commandments for the present day. He unfurled the scroll. It was a poster.

COMING SOON

FOR THE SECOND TIME IN TWO THOUSAND YEARS

THE ONE AND ONLY JESUS CHRIST

"Whadaya think?" asked Hiram, as Father Sorrell sank slowly to the floor.

* * *

"What is it you're playing now, dear?" Mary Mog squinted down at the computer screen.

"I told you last time, mother, this is not a game." God pressed a key to remove the picture from the screen; Rabbit World was not a fit sight for someone as innocent as His mother, especially since the Rabbits had recently discovered bondage. "It's a management tool, a sophisticated model for decision making."

"Oh," said Mary, disappointed, "I thought perhaps it was Sonic the Hedgehog. I've always fancied a go on that."

Taking advantage of Hiram's temporary absence, she'd agreed to accompany Peter and Paul on a visit to God, in the hope that they could appeal to His better nature.

She watched God as He flicked through the various worlds. "Whatever it is, can't you spare a few moments for your old mum?"

God sighed and turned to her. "I've told you before, mother, I do have work to do." His voice softened as He looked at her pleading face. "Go on then, what is it?"

"We're worried about what's going on in Heaven. This Hiram doesn't seem to know what he's doing. Don't get me wrong, dear, I've nothing against him, he's a very nice man. It's just that, well, since you've been gone, the place has been falling apart."

She told Him about the increased level of complaints, especially from Heaven-dwellers. Peter and Paul joined in, complaining about Hiram's endless round of reorganisations.

"He's empire-building," said Peter. "And what worries me is that it's not supposed to be his empire in the first place. We're asking, no, we're begging you to return and put everything back to normal."

"Don't you trust me, Peter? Have I ever let you down?"

"Well . . . " Peter frowned.

"Go on," said God, "spit it out."

"We were a bit miffed when you went and got yourself crucified."

"Case in point. Now you know there's a good reason for everything I do. You'll just have to trust me again." God turned back to His computer.

* * *

"I've been wondering," said Gabriel, "whether we've been short-changed."

"What do you mean?" asked Raphael. They were sitting on the coach waiting for the appointed time at which the angels would return.

"Well, just think about it. We go on strike, submit a list of demands,

94

and Bob's your uncle, the Trust gives in without any discussion. Now, have you ever, in the history of industrial relations, heard of that happening before?"

"No," replied Raphael, munching an egg and cress sandwich. "Now you come to mention it, I can't say that I have. You know that course in personnel management I went on?"

Gabriel nodded.

"As part of that, we studied industrial relations and you're quite right, it was all conflict, negotiation and arbitration. No mention of out-and-out capitulation. You're right, something smells fishy."

"Talking of smell," said Gabriel, eyeing Raphael's sandwich with distaste.

"You wouldn't begrudge me my favourite sandwich, would you? This," he said, taking another bite, "is what I call Heaven on Earth."

"To go back to my point," said Gabriel, "we'd better have another think. There may be something else we should have asked for. Management gave in far too easily." He looked out of the window and spotted the angels on their way back. "Maybe we'll talk about this later."

* * *

There was a man who walked the streets of Heaven. He hadn't been there long, although he had been dead for many hundreds of years.

This man was very bitter. He wished that, all those years ago, they had sent him straight to Hell. It was what he had expected. Instead, they had put him in Purgatory. Although it wasn't Hell, it wasn't far off it. In Purgatory, every hour seemed like a day; every day like a month. The years dragged on and on, years of tedium and endless organised prayer, in later years there was the chance of parole; but the build up of hope was inevitably followed by intense disappointment.

When the gates of Purgatory had finally opened for him, Judas Iscariot had been filled with hope for the last, the very last time. He had been punished and now he was to be forgiven. He prepared himself for the reunion with Jesus, ready to humiliate himself and beg for forgiveness.

But Judas came out into a place where hardly anybody remembered who he was. There was no-one waiting outside the prison gates, no-one to gather him back into the fold. The freedom that he'd craved for so long was not a personal gesture from Jesus, it was a blanket amnesty to all the inmates of Purgatory. And, as for Jesus, He wasn't even around any more.

So Judas Iscariot walked the streets of Heaven like a tramp; bearded, shabby and unrecognised; brooding, hating, uttering bitter curses to anyone who would listen.

Now a hatred brewed so dark, so bitter, could not go unheard by certain ears – ears trained to detect any thought or utterance directed against God, even in Heaven. The very existence of a malignant thought opened up a channel of communication to the Devil.

As Judas shuffled through the streets of Heaven, a seductive voice penetrated through into his rambling mind.

"Judas, I know you can hear me, Judas. I have heard you, a voice crying in the wilderness."

Judas stopped walking. "Who is speaking? I know that voice, I know it of old." People walking on the pavement crossed to the other side of the road to avoid the madman who was talking to himself.

The Devil laughed. "Yes, Judas. You know me, I have spoken to you before. How long has it been? It must be nearly two thousand years. You should have come to me then, Judas, I would have been proud to have you. You know what they say; better to reign in Hell. You could have been my left hand man. Perhaps . . . " He paused. "Perhaps, it's not too late. Open your mind to me, Judas, let me penetrate that fog, let me unravel that mess, then I will tell you how we can join together to defeat a common enemy."

* * *

It had been a successful visit for Hiram. He'd started to lay down the foundations, plant a few seeds in the right places, but he could see that he would have to take things gently. There was so much scepticism to penetrate.

As the coach started up, Hiram felt something tugging at him, it was almost a physical pain, telling him that there was something he'd left behind, something linking him to Earth, but try as he did, he couldn't imagine what. He had been on Earth just long enough for the Heaven-induced amnesia to start to lose its hold on him, but not long enough for the memories to return. He shrugged. Whatever it was would have to wait until his next visit.

Tracey, meanwhile, was still glowing with pleasure. Earth had been everything she'd imagined it to be, and more. Once she'd got over her anxiety about the young man who'd stolen her questionnaire, she was intrigued and started to look more closely at the other young men who came her way. Many of them were as beautiful as him to look at, and most of them looked at her in the same way as he had, but only for a few brief moments until the interview started. Then, their eyes would glaze over and they seemed to stare straight through her. There had definitely been something different about that young man. Tracey wondered if it could possibly be that special thing she so enjoyed reading about: love at first sight. If only she knew his name, she could carve it on trees: Tracey loves ? As the coach sped towards Heaven, it didn't matter anymore that she didn't know his name; his face and, eventually, his very existence faded gradually from her memory. But the memory of Earth itself did not fade, and Tracey was left with the certainty that she had missed out on something good.

The black limousine followed the convoy until it reached Route 666, the turning for Hell.

* * *

Julia sat alone at a table in the Ambrosia Coffee Bar, stirring her tea. The visit to her parents had been easier than expected. Heaven had mellowed them and they'd been delighted to see her. She couldn't help laughing at their appearance. Although physically they both looked as they must have done in their mid-twenties, they dressed as they had done in their last years. Julia's mother wore an old faded pinafore over a polo neck jumper, and her father sat with his crimplene trousers held up by braces, and the sleeves of his nylon shirt rolled up to his elbows. It had been an incongruous image.

Julia had gone back to the office to find a new pile of petitions and complaints, referred via the Heavenly Hotline. So much for taking a short break while Hiram was away.

"You'll go straight through the bottom of that cup if you're not careful," a familiar voice interrupted. "Don't mind if we join you, do you?" Maggie and Martha sat down. "Is there something wrong?" asked Maggie.

"I just don't understand why we're getting so many complaints." Julia looked up. "There seems to be so much unhappiness up here."

"I know exactly what you mean, but it hasn't always been like this, has it Martha?"

Martha shook her head.

Maggie continued. "It started going downhill when God left. Don't get me wrong, I'm not blaming your boss or the Trust, they are doing their best, but they're only men, after all. They lack the intuition and sensitivity that a woman would bring to the job. That's what I liked about God, He was never afraid to express His feminine

98

side, to show compassion. Now, if Hiram could be made to realise that, and involve women more in the running of Heaven . . ."

"You're never satisfied," Martha said. "I thought you'd be happy now you're a director."

"I was, but can't you see that it still isn't enough? As a Director, I get to run my department and I can make recommendations to the Trust, but I want to be able to make the decisions. If they think that they can keep me quiet by giving me this job, they've got another thing coming." She looked at Julia. "You must be close to Hiram, you're from his time, perhaps you could make him understand."

"I don't know," Julia said, "I haven't been working for him long enough to talk to him on that level." She felt uncomfortable, knowing that she had Maggie to thank for finding her the job, but at the same time she owed her loyalty to her employer.

"Shame on you, Maggie," Martha said. "You can't expect the poor girl to plead your cause for you."

"We girls have to stick together," said Maggie. "Anyway, it would only take a subtle hint or two. We women are good at that sort of thing, just point him in the right direction, then next thing, he'll be claiming that it was all his idea. Besides," she winked, "I'd be surprised if Julia hasn't already been doing a spot of lobbying of her own."

"What do you mean?" asked Julia.

"Surely you've taken the opportunity to discuss your marital difficulties with Hiram?"

"No." Julia looked shocked. "It would be unprofessional to use my position to advance my own interests. Besides, I'm not sure if I want to be reunited with my husband anymore."

"But think about all the other people in that situation, why don't you do it to help them? I understand your reservations, but it wouldn't be as if you were influencing Hiram against his own judgement. You know Hiram, he's full of liberal ideas, but not very observant. He's a reasonable man, but he needs to have these problems brought to his attention before he can do something about them." She smiled. "You mark my words, he'll thank you for telling him."

* * *

The Daily Sphere
SPY CAMERA – MISSING COACH MYSTERY
Police examining film from motorway surveillance
cameras for clues to last week's multiple motorbike
crash on the M1 are reported to be puzzled as to why an
executive passenger coach appears on film from only
one of the two cameras situated between exits 8 and 9.
Technicians are checking the equipment for faults. In the
meantime, police are investigating the suggestion that
this was the same coach that went missing weeks ago,
along with its fifty-two Japanese passengers and driver.

* * *

Torquemada, his eyes burning with fanaticism, stared down at the accused heretic who lay tethered to the table. He picked up the iron rod and moved, slowly and deliberately, to the brazier and thrust the rod in. Carefully calculated minutes later, he drew out the white-hot rod and moved back towards his terrified victim. By the time he reached him, the rod had cooled down. With a sigh of resignation, Torquemada the Tortoise turned for the umpteenth time and headed again towards the brazier.

The Satan virus moved on.

* * *

The Devil lay resplendent on his chaise longue upholstered with black satin, a genial smile on his lips as he scanned the latest batch of newcomers. They were the usual motley crew: psychopaths, drug dealers, politicians and High Court judges, their facial expressions ranging from curiosity to sheer terror. The Devil began his welcome speech in a voice that was warm and reassuring. "Welcome, my faithful subjects," he held out his arms in a gesture of friendliness, "welcome to my domain. Please, do not be frightened, you are among friends now. Make yourselves comfortable, my servants will bring you refreshments." He paused while scantily clad lovelies, male and female, led the newcomers to couches covered with plump, black velvet cushions and brought them dishes of succulent fruit and goblets of strong wine.

The Devil walked among his new subjects, smiling paternally. "I have no doubt," he continued, "that you will have heard all manner of terrifying stories about this place. Fiery pits, where demons with pitchforks torment you, dark dungeons equipped with instruments of torture." He laughed. "Black propaganda, my friends, put about by the other side. I admit, there are torture chambers here, but the use of these facilities is voluntary, solely for those among us, and there are many, who derive their pleasure from either inflicting or receiving pain. Think about it logically. It would hardly be in my best interests to mistreat my loyal subjects, would it? The good Doctor Faustus can bear witness to that. How goes it, Doctor Faustus?"

"Very well," a voice piped from the corner. "It was all my own fault, you know. We did a deal, fair and square, my soul for twenty-four years of having everything I asked for, of being waited on hand and foot by demons." He smiled weakly. "The contract was properly signed, in my own blood, but when it came to the time for me to pay up, I tried to renege on the deal. I deserved everything I got – and I think being torn asunder by demons was a small price to pay for such treachery. And they were kind enough to sew me back together again." His eyes watered at the memory. "Now, I'm as good as new and everything is hunky dory."

"Thank you, Doctor. That will be enough," said Satan. "Now, my friends, refresh yourselves, then my helpers will take you on a tour of the facilities here." And with a gracious bow, he left the room.

"Tell me," a young American woman asked one of the demon hostesses, "is there a Mrs Satan?"

The demon laughed and shook her head.

"Oh, don't tell me he's gay. It would be such a waste."

"It's not that, madam. He's omnisexual."

"What do you mean?"

The demon waitress leant forward and whispered, "He'll screw anything that moves." She paused, then added, "And a lot of things that don't."

"I think I'm going to like it here." The woman shivered deliciously.

The demon waitress smiled to herself, knowingly. What Satan had told his new subjects was, in essence, true. There was no torture, at least, not for the wicked. There was a special induction course for those people who still retained an element of goodness in their souls – a gruelling course, watching endless video nasties, in conjunction with a constant round of drunkenness alternating with ferocious hangovers and, for light relief, long sessions of group torture. As Satan would say, you've got to be cruel to be kind. Because, for anyone not totally evil, Hell would be like, well, it would be like Hell.

But, although there was no fiery pit, no demons with pitchforks (except in the Hellfire Club, and that was just for show, and of course for the barbecue), the problem with Hell was that there was nothing nice there. Even the delicious fruit and wine that the new inmates were now enjoying was rotten and maggot-ridden under its veneer of illusion. The beautiful young men and women who were now pandering to their every whim were, in reality, foul

102

smelling demons with scaly skin and rotting teeth. The illusion would last only until the inmates had entered the inner gates of Hell. Once inside, they would have to get used to the reality. Unlike Heaven, the illusory powers of Hell were limited and therefore available only for special occasions.

* * *

The Devil left the reception area and headed for his private chambers to await the return of the faithful Beelzebub. He did not have to wait long, but was dismayed to see his most trusted servant carried in on a stretcher.

"What's happened?" he raged.

"Church," gasped Beelzebub, in between snatched breaths. "Can't speak."

"You must convalesce, old friend. We'll talk later, when you are well." The Devil snapped his fingers for service. "Take him down to the dungeons and have a black mass said over him. That's the best cure for church sickness."

As Beelzebub muttered his thanks, he was borne away by a host of demons.

The Devil turned to Jake, who stood in a corner, trying very hard not to shake with terror. He'd rarely been so close to the Big Boss.

"Well," said the Devil, "can you shed any light on this?"

"I'm not sure what happened to him, your Satanic Majesty. When we met back at the limo he was in a bad way, he just kept muttering something about 'posters'."

"Posters?" The Devil frowned.

"Yes, sir. I'm afraid I couldn't make out anything else he said. Apart from the J word." He blushed.

"The J word? Come on, spit it out, we're not afraid to say that word here. What on Earth do they teach you at Demon School nowadays? Come on, say it."

"Jesus," blurted the demon, "he kept saying 'Jesus'."

"Thank you," said the Devil firmly. "That wasn't too bad, now, was it? You haven't been turned into a flower or a fluffy bunny or anything else sickeningly nice, have you?"

"No, sir." Jake shook his head, then quickly added, "I did find out something about what the angels are up to." He held out the questionnaire. "They were stopping people in the streets and asking them these questions."

"Very interesting," said the Devil, casting his eye over it. "You did well to get hold of one of these. I am pleased with you." He snapped his fingers again. "Prepare a feast for my good servant Jake, to celebrate his promotion to Demon Second Class."

Jake bowed. "You are very kind, your majesty."

The Devil nodded graciously. "Enjoy yourself, Jake, you have deserved it."

* * *

"Have you ever been in love?" Tracey asked Julia, as the curtains closed on the Paradise Theatre's latest production of Romeo and Juliet.

"Yes." Julia looked nervously at the little angel, wondering what sort of question would be coming next. She had no idea whether the rudimentary vocational education that Tracey had received would have covered the facts of life. She had never been a mother, had no experience of dealing with questions of that nature, but prepared herself to cope with this new responsibility.

"Is it as wonderful as it is in the books?" Tracey's eyes, trusting and appealing, gazed up at Julia's.

"Well, I suppose so." Julia paused as she waged an internal debate over whether she should tell the truth. She assumed that in Heaven, at least for angels if not for ordinary citizens like herself, love probably was just like it was described in romantic novels. She opted for an edited version of the truth. "Yes, I was very happy with my husband, down on Earth."

To Julia's relief, Tracey was satisfied with that. Let her believe, thought Julia bitterly, that love is never about betrayal and deep, deep, disappointment. Let her enjoy her illusions, for she will never discover the reality.

* * *

No-one took any notice of the man who crouched down in the corner of the common room of the New Limbo Hostel, tugging at his matted beard. The voice was here again, drilling into his head.

"Is it any wonder that you feel bitter, Judas? You were simply thrown away, used and discarded, left to fester for two thousand years. Yes, think about it, Judas. They needed you to betray Jesus, to help create the legend. It was predestined, you had no choice. Remember that last meal at the Mount of Olives Kebab House in Jerusalem, when Jesus foretold that you would betray him? Think about it, Judas. He knew what was going to happen, He could have stopped it, but he didn't. It was all planned, down to the last detail. You were just a cog in the wheel, driven helplessly by the big engines. You were the betrayed, Judas, not the betrayer. And you're not the only one, I was a victim, too. All I did was try to show a bit of initiative, a little ambition, and I was cast out, just like that. No warning, no right of appeal, we had no trade unions in those days. Then after, I got to thinking, who put those ideas in my head in the first place? I'd been quite happy in Heaven, no cares, no worries, then something started to niggle at me, telling me that I wasn't appreciated, that I could do better for myself. Then I figured it out, God decided He needed a foil, a symbol of evil, and I ended up as the fall guy. Like you, I had no choice in the matter. Like you, I was just there, in the wrong place, at the wrong time. Let me into

105

your head, Judas, together we can wreak revenge, we can fight for justice."

Slowly the clouds in Judas's eyes dispersed, to be replaced with a piercing clarity. But no-one noticed the change, because no-one looked at the tramp, who sat in a corner, muttering to himself.

* * *

"How are you feeling, Beelzebub old friend? Are you sure you're well enough to talk about it?"

"Yes, your Lowness," said Beelzebub, weakly. "I think I will feel better once I've got it off my chest."

"Take your time, old friend. Fancy a grape?" The Devil offered a paper bag. "They're black, your favourite."

A uniformed nurse appeared and shook her head. "Can't you read?" she asked, pointing to a sign at the end of the bed, "NIL BY MOUTH".

"Sorry, sister." Satan scowled at the disappearing figure of the nurse.

"Liquid diet only, I'm afraid," Beelzebub said, nodding towards the black tube, which fed blood into his veins. "In a couple of days I'll be allowed to drink it from a glass." He smiled faintly.

"Just don't overdo things," the Devil said, munching a grape. "Take as long as you need to get well, you know I'll keep your job open for you."

"Thank you, sir. I am anxious to get back as soon as possible, though. That American, he's up to something good. I followed him, every step of the way." He shuddered. "To four churches, one cathedral and one archbishop's residence." His eyes watered. "It was awful."

"Yes, I can imagine," said the Devil, trying to hide his impatience. "What is he up to?"

"It's just as you feared, sir. The Second Coming."

106

"On the contrary, Beelzebub, I see it as an opportunity. Did he say when it is to be?"

"No, your majesty, but the posters say 'COMING SOON'. I tried to bring you one, but the priest, he put it on the altar. I just couldn't bring myself . . ."

"There, there," said Satan soothingly. "Don't upset yourself. What you've done is above and beyond the call of duty. I want you to rest now, get yourself fit and don't worry." He leant forward and whispered in his ear, "I have a spy in the enemy camp, Beelzebub."

The demon's eyes widened. "In Heaven?"

The Devil nodded. "I'll tell you more when you're better. I will go now, that dragon of a nurse is scowling at me. If she wasn't doing such a wonderful job of looking after you, I'd have her sizzling on a spit. Still," he smiled, "plenty of time for that when you're recovered."

CHAPTER 7

"These survey results are very interesting." Hiram was studying the statistics that Julia and her team of helpers had prepared from the completed forms. "It's pretty much what I expected – people want different things but they fall into distinct groups. The romantics – the ones who wanna spend eternity with their loved ones."

Julia looked up, wondering if this would be a good time to speak, but the words caught in her throat.

"Then there's the fantasists," Hiram continued, "the dreamers. The ones who wanna play for the LA Dodgers in the World Series, for England in the World Cup, or join Eric Clapton on-stage. The hedonists, who long for a life of sensual pleasure, great sex, food and drink, without the more unpleasant consequences. Then the spiritualists, the seekers of knowledge and enlightenment, who wanna sit down with God and discuss the meaning of life." He shook his head. "I guess they may be disappointed."

"Don't you think He'll come back?"

"Well I reckon He'd be back in a flash if He wasn't happy with the way things were going. I guess I must be doing OK so far." He smiled, turned to the next page of statistics, and frowned. "Then there's the sad, lonely people who just want someone to love, or a baby."

"Perhaps they could look after the Limbo Babies," Julia piped in. She was thinking of Tracey's stolen childhood.

"Yeah, and we can give 'em coaching in social skills, therapy, counselling." He paused, thoughtfully.

"I know this might sound like a silly question . . ." began Julia.

"Go on."

"You haven't asked the people who live here what they want, have you?"

"No, I just assumed that if there was a problem, we'd know about it."

"I hate to remind you, but that's what you said about the angels."

Hiram nodded slowly. "You got something there."

"Besides," said Julia, as she stood up and walked over to her desk, "we've now got evidence to show that not everybody is happy up here." She placed a computer print-out in front of Hiram, a thick wad of paper containing hundreds of pages.

"What's this?" Hiram frowned.

"This is all that's been transmitted by electronic mail since you computerised the Heavenly Helpline. These are all the complaints and petitions that have been referred to you as Chief Executive."

"Can't the departments handle these?" said Hiram, flicking through the pages in horror. Obviously he wasn't doing such a great job.

"No, they all relate to corporate policies, the ones that come from the top." Julia felt her confidence growing. "Like the one that says only the first marriage counts, and that people who married widows, widowers or divorcees have no rights."

"I didn't even know that existed," protested Hiram.

"Well, it does," said Julia, as she turned the pages of the print-out to show Hiram the list of letters and petitions from the Society for the Promotion of Rights for the Remarried. "I was invited to join that organisation, Hiram, because I'm a second wife."

"I see," said Hiram. This was a real teaser. "But surely, to make all these people happy would be at the expense of all the first wives and husbands."

"All they're asking for," said Julia, "is the opportunity to reach a compromise, to share partners if necessary. Given that time is supposed to be an inexhaustible resource up here, I wouldn't have thought that unreasonable."

"I guess not," said Hiram, but he wasn't convinced. "It's something we'll have to give some thought to. In the meantime, you've convinced me of one thing, that we do need to consult Heaven's citizens. It'll be interesting to check out their views with those of people on Earth. I'm glad you raised the matter, Julia."

She smiled, Maggie had been right. "By the way," said Julia, "there's a tramp who's been hanging around the building recently. I've noticed him a few times."

"Yeah," said Hiram. "I saw him. He's probably just bumming around for a while – to see what it's like. I don't know why he'd want to dress like that, though."

"Maybe, but there's something about him I don't like – as if he's watching and waiting for something." She shuddered.

"Julia, you're still using Earthly references to judge people by. This is Heaven, what harm can he do? He's probably some great philosopher who's just creating a bit of space for himself. Hey, if you're really worried, I'll have a word with Saint Alexis, he's patron saint of down and outs. Maybe he knows something about this guy."

* * *

"Back and forth, up and down like bloody yo-yos," said Gabriel.

"What do you mean?" Raphael asked.

"Well, first he sends us down to Earth to ask these questions, then we've got to ask them all over again up here, then he says we'll be going back down to Earth soon. It isn't good for us, it's not natural. Several of the angels got travel sick on the journey and, worst of all, it's unsettled them. They're giving Earth a sort of cult status and showing off to the others who haven't been there. Look at that lot, for instance."

He pointed to a group of young angels, all of whom had adopted

110

some of the fashions they'd seen on Earth. Baseball caps worn back to front, oversized sweatshirts and torn jeans were the favourite styles; but there was one angel who had been so impressed by a punk he'd interviewed that he'd dyed his wings pink and green and pierced his nose. Seeing the archangels' disapproving stares, the youngsters pulled faces and then ran off.

"That's another thing they've picked up down there, a lack of respect for their elders and betters. Oh, I can see now why Hiram gave in so easily. He knew that all this to-ing and fro-ing would make our work more difficult and that he'd get more than his money's worth from us."

"But he doesn't pay us anything." Raphael wrinkled his brow.

"I was talking metaphorically, you dickhead."

"No need to take it out on me," Raphael sniffed. "I can't understand what it is you want, anyway. What more can we ask for?"

"I've thought about that," said Gabriel proudly. "We are going to submit a new set of demands, we'll ask for longer holidays and an area of Heaven to be set aside purely for our use, so that we can get away from the hoi-polloi."

"Will we have to go on strike again?"

"Not if we can avoid it. Last time, I had complaints from angels about the amount of extra work they had to do to repair the damage caused by the strike. No, I thought we'd try a work to rule this time. We'll continue to maintain the fabric of Heaven, but we'll refuse to undertake any of this additional work until we get the extra holiday entitlements we ask for."

* * *

"Give us a break, Lucy. Just sit down and talk."

"I'm busy!" Lucy declared, furiously dusting away the dust that had no business being there, the dust that she'd created and would

111

re-create, as soon as she'd got rid of it.

"Suit yourself." The Angel Gloria swung her legs round, resting her feet provocatively on the arm of the settee. Lucy tutted and conjured up a matching set of embroidered arm covers for the suite, one of which appeared under Gloria's feet. Gloria lit a cigarette and dangled the burning end threateningly over Lucy's spotless cream carpet. Lucy knelt at her side, holding an ashtray she'd hurriedly brought into existence under the cigarette.

"Well, that'll do, I suppose," said Gloria. "At least I've managed to stop you dashing about for the time being. Now, if I promise to behave, will you sit down quietly and listen?"

Lucy sat stiffbacked in the armchair, a scowl on her face, while Gloria sat up and extinguished her cigarette.

"That's better, girl," she said. "There's no reason why we shouldn't be friendly, after all, we both want the same thing, you back together with your ever-loving husband."

"I find that hard to believe," snapped Lucy, "since you've been spending long, cosy nights in the shed with him. Do your superiors know what you get up to? Disgusting, I call it." She folded her arms.

Gloria laughed. "If that wasn't so funny, I'd be insulted. Me and your Martin? Do me a favour."

"And just what is wrong with my husband?" Lucy demanded. "I'll have you know that he was considered quite a catch."

"By your standards, perhaps. Don't look so indignant, I didn't mean it as an insult. It's just that we angels never mate with humans." She wrinkled her nose in disgust. "Believe me, honey," Gloria puffed out her chest and patted her hair, "Once you've had an angel, you don't want to be bothered with the lower life forms."

"If you're so superior, what are you doing waiting on us?" Lucy smirked.

"For the same reasons that you lot keep animals as pets, train them in circuses, clean up their shit, I suppose. It keeps us amused."

"I don't have to listen to this." Lucy stood up again.

"Sit down!" As Gloria spoke, Lucy found herself pushed back down by unseen hands. "I don't want to prolong this conversation any more than you do. What I want is for you to give your husband and me a break. I'm sick to the teeth of playing nursemaid. The sooner you stop sulking and take him back, the sooner I can get on with my life. I have got better things to do, you know." She paused. "Go on, give it a try. There's nothing to stop you making him suffer a bit more before you forgive him, if that's what you want. Well, what do you say, shall I go and fetch him?"

Lucy nodded miserably and Gloria went out into the garden. But the shed was empty, Martin was nowhere to be seen. "Oh, bugger," she said aloud.

* * *

There was a man standing at the back of the meeting hall. No-one noticed him – to be more exact, they went out of their way not to notice him. He was a filthy-looking tramp with a long, matted beard and staring eyes. Had anyone troubled to look into the man's eyes they would have seen a multitude of lost souls staring out at them.

It was a public meeting, convened by Hiram to tell the citizens about the questionnaires that would soon be dropping through the front door of every household in Heaven. It was a customer satisfaction survey, Hiram was explaining, to give citizens the opportunity to have their say about the services provided for them and about the future direction that Heaven should take.

Judas Iscariot, and the being who inhabited him, watched together through Judas' eyes and listened through Judas' ears.

Near the front of the hall, a group of archangels were gathered together. "It's just a public relations exercise," whispered Gabriel to his colleagues, as they listened to Hiram's speech. "He's not

113

really interested in what people up here want. They're a captive audience. This is all for the benefit of those yet to come, turning Heaven into a tourist attraction. And have you realised that the more people who come up here, the more work there'll be for the likes of us?"

Hiram was still speaking, assuring the citizens of Heaven that their views would be taken into account when formulating any proposals for the reorganisation of Heaven and that they would be consulted again before any decisions were made.

"Let's have a word with him now," Gabriel said at the end of the meeting, as billions of people filed smoothly and swiftly past. Together they approached Hiram, who was now speaking to the other trustees. He turned to them. "Hi there. Glad you could come along."

"Yes, we were very interested in this meeting," Gabriel said. "It's nice to hear that you place so much importance on consultation. What a shame that you didn't see fit to discuss your proposals with us first."

"Is there a problem?"

"The problem is that you don't seem to appreciate that these plans of yours mean extra work for the angels, with no extra reward."

"So, what are you asking for?"

Gabriel recited the angels' demands. "And if you don't agree," he added, "we'll be working to rule, which means no delivering and collecting questionnaires, no collating statistics, and definitely no going back down to Earth."

Hiram looked at the archangels thoughtfully. "Sure, seems reasonable," he said. He sought out one particular face in the group of archangels. "Raphael, you're Director of Personnel now, draw me up a report on the staffing implications of increasing the vacation entitlement. I guess we could recruit and train additional staff. Perhaps some of the ordinary citizens of Heaven would like to join the workforce if there aren't enough angels." He looked back at

114

Gabriel. "Then I suggest you meet with the Director of Planning about designating a zone for you, and if you need any help to design the place, I'll make sure that's forthcoming. I'll speak to Saint Thomas for you if you like, ask him to put his people at your disposal."

He smiled warmly at the archangels before turning back to the Trustees.

Gabriel glared at him and stormed from the stage, followed by the others.

"What's wrong?" asked Michael. "He's given us what we wanted, hasn't he?"

Gabriel stopped in his tracks. "Are you lot too thick to see what he's up to? He's trying to make us look stupid, that's what, and he's laughing at us. Don't be fooled by that sickly smile of his, it's really a smirk. And as for you," he turned on Raphael, "all this 'draw me up a report' business, he's trying to set us against each other. Well, it won't wash with me. I'm going back now to check on the union rules. There must be something we can get him on, there must be a rule against an employer not oppressing the workforce, it's just not natural."

* * *

God didn't dare take His eyes off the screen. The Dogs had discovered interplanetary travel and were pointing their first manned, or rather, dogged, rocket "Leica I" at Cat World. It would be utter carnage. God was sorry, He had been rather fond of the Dogs.

"You sent for me, Lord?" Hiram said, coming up beside Him.

"I did? Ah, yes. I've been thinking about this appearance on Earth. Christmas Day would seem appropriate. Don't you think?"

"Yeah, I like it. Has a neatness about it. Have you decided on the venue?"

"Yes, everywhere. I will be everywhere."

115

"Gee, why didn't I think of it myself? Simultaneous, satellite-linked television broadcasts, great!"

God looked at Hiram oddly, but said nothing.

"And where would you like to transmit from, Lord? I think it's real important that you put on a show in front of a live audience, a few miracles, that sort of thing. If you restrict your appearance to television only, the sceptics will put it down to camera tricks."

"If you like, it's all the same to me. What about the Hollywood Bowl?"

A look of pain flitted across Hiram's face at the memory of his last moments on Earth. "Whatever you say, Lord," he said, stoically.

God slapped him on the back. "Lighten up, Hiram. I was only kidding. Have you any suggestions?"

Hiram cleared his throat. "There's Earls Court, Wembley, the National Exhibition Centre. Whadaya say to an international whistle-stop tour?"

"No," said God, gently. "Once will be enough, believe me. What about Earls Court?"

"OK, it's your party."

"Yes, I suppose it is. After all, it will be my birthday, although few people seem to remember that."

"I guess that after this year no-one will ever forget that again," said Hiram. "Now, we've got some great ideas for promoting the show; merchandise, for example, albums, T-shirts, badges . . ."

God turned from His screen. "Well, Hiram, you know I don't like mixing religion and business . . .

"Hey, I was thinking of freebies."

"That's all right, then."

Hiram felt pleased with himself. "So, we've agreed the date and venue, is it OK to get started?"

"Yes, go ahead," said God.

* * *

116

Julia walked into her office. It was dark, which was unusual, with dim light from a flickering streetlamp filtering in through half open blinds. She could just make out the outline of someone sitting in the chair, in a reclining position, with feet on the desk. The intruder was wearing a fedora and smoking a French cigarette. The swirls of grey smoke hung in layers, illuminated at regular intervals by the dim light.

"I let myself in, d'ya mind?" The voice was low and husky.

"Who are you?" asked Julia.

"I'm from the G.A.'s office." A wallet skidded across the desk. Julia picked it up and read, "Gloria – Licensed Guardian Angel". Julia raised an eyebrow.

"I'm investigating the case of a missing person." Gloria switched on the desk light. Julia shielded her eyes. "Sorry," said Gloria. She adjusted the light.

Julia studied the angel, a brunette; the hat didn't stop her hair falling halfway across her face like a curtain. She wore a dark mackintosh with the collar turned up.

"When did you last see your husband, Mrs Davis?"

"It was a while ago," said Julia. "At the hostel, I was at a meeting. He turned up to see me. I told him it was over. I haven't seen him since. I take it he's your missing person?"

"Yep. He seems to have vanished off the face of Heaven, Mrs Davis. Hey, did anyone ever tell you how much you look like the other one? The first Mrs Davis? You could be sisters."

Julia said nothing.

Gloria continued. "I don't know how much you know about guardian angels, Mrs Davis?"

"I'd prefer it if you called me Julia."

"Sure. Well, Julia, I'm Martin's G.A., and I'm linked to him by an invisible bond. That way, I know when he's headed for trouble. It also means that, wherever he is, I should be able to find him. Instantly. But I can't. I'm pulling the invisible thread and the other end is cut, clean off. There's no blip on my celestial radar." She paused to take a long drag on her cigarette. "So I go see Saint Anthony at the Lost and Found Bureau. He can't find any trace either. So I start to get worried. Then I think of you."

Julia shrugged. "What makes you think I know where he is?"

Gloria stood up, walked to the window and parted the blinds with her fingers. "If I can't find him, there are only two possibilities. He could be somewhere out of my reach, but there's only one place that can be, Hell, and I pray he isn't there. The only other option is that he's being sheltered by a greater power than mine. That's why I came to you. You seem to have found yourself some pretty powerful friends lately. Are you hiding him, Julia?"

"No, and if you'll excuse me, I have work to do." Julia stood up and opened the office door. Gloria ground out her cigarette on the desk top and walked to the door. "Here's my card. If he gets in touch, call me." She paused. "You don't seem too worried about your husband, Julia, if you don't mind my saying."

"Like I said, it's all over between us. I told him to go back to Lucy. Besides, this is Heaven, what harm could he come to?"

Gloria raised her eyebrows and strolled out of the office.

From her office window, Julia watched until Gloria had left the building and was out of sight, then put on her coat. She would go back to the hostel, just in case Martin had left a message for her there. She hoped that she had managed to convince the angel that she had no further interest in her husband. If Martin had gone into hiding, then surely he would try to make contact with her. She didn't want to lead Lucy or the angel to him. If he'd been prepared to take such a drastic step for her sake, then perhaps there was still a chance for them.

As she left Eternity Hall, Julia was too preoccupied to notice the tramp who was lurking in the corridor a few feet away from her office, and who watched her walk briskly out before he slipped in through the office door.

* * *

"Your ideas are so wonderful, Hiram." Maggie gazed deep into his eyes as they sat over cocktails in a booth in the American bar. "In fact, you've inspired me. It's only a teensy-weensy little idea, but I thought you might just want to consider it."

"Sure," said Hiram, "I'm all ears."

"Well . . . " She sat back suddenly, and shook her head. "No, it's too silly."

Hiram covered her hand with his. "Please, I wanna hear it. I'm sure it won't be silly."

"Well," she began again, "I was thinking that albums and T-shirts are great for the young generation, but perhaps we need something different for the adults."

Hiram nodded. "Yeah, I see where you're coming from. Whadaya have in mind?"

"Well," she wriggled a little, "I don't know if you've heard that the perfumers have made me their patron saint. Now, I know I've done nothing to deserve the honour, it's almost too embarrassing to mention really, but I did wonder if we could perhaps launch a new perfume, 'Maggie', and give that away to the ladies. And we could make a matching aftershave, called 'Hiram' for the men." She raised her eyebrows playfully.

Hiram nodded again. "Reckon you might've hit on something there, although I'm not convinced that men would go for a cologne called after me. But the basic idea's neat. We could market the range under the name 'Heaven Scent'. Hey, this calls for another drink."

On his way back with the drinks, Hiram spotted Gabriel and his friends, who had just stopped by for a drink. He smiled and nodded at them before rejoining Maggie.

"Well, lookee over there," said Gabriel. "That smug bastard, he really gets up my nose."

"I still don't understand you," Raphael said. "He's agreed to everything we've asked for so far."

"Yes, and I know why he's doing it. He's stopping us from exercising our democratic right to take legitimate industrial action." Gabriel took a long gulp of his beer. "I've a good mind to go over there and wipe the smile right off his face."

"Come on," said Michael, "have you seen who he's with? If I'd just got off with the best looking babe in Heaven, I'd be smiling."

"Typical woman," said Gabriel, "going for the Yank with the biggest bank balance. Let's go to the other bar, I don't like the smell in here."

* * *

"I've called this special meeting of the Trust, Hiram, because I think it's about time you told us what you've been up to." Peter looked over to his fellow Trustees for support. "You're continuing to railroad plans through that we know nothing about."

"I'm sorry, guys. I guess I just got over-excited. I see a job that needs doing and I get on with it. But you're right, I owe you an apology and I'll do my damnedest from now on to keep you informed."

"You can start," said Paul, "by giving us a report on the trip to Earth."

"Well, guys, what can I say? It was a real useful trip. I've made contact with several clergymen; members of the Anglican and Catholic churches in London, all held in high respect."

"I think you've gone about things the wrong way here," said Peter. "We've got proper channels set up for contacting the clergy. You should have checked with us first and we'd have sent an official delegation to the Pope."

"I like to get the troops on my side before I deal with the generals," said Hiram. Some of the Trustees exchanged glances. They were aware that Hiram used these tactics in Heaven; after all, why else had he created so many new executive posts and given in to all the angels' demands?

"And put the generals' backs up in the process. You'll have to put it right on your next visit, as a matter of priority." Peter insisted.

"OK, I guess." Hiram continued, "Besides, I'll have to speak to the top brass to sort out the funding. We need to pay in advance for the hire of the venue, for staff, and we need to advertise in Earth's press on top of the promotion we'll be doing. I'm gonna ask the churches to put up fifty per cent of the money, and I'll come up with the rest."

"How are you going to manage that?" asked Peter.

"Hey, I was a rich man, in my own right. I used my fortune to start up my ministry and there's still a lot left. It's all in a trust fund, controlled by . . ." He paused. "Funny, I can't seem to remember who the executor is, but I'm sure it's someone I would trust with my own life. It'll come back to me. All I need to do is to get in contact with the person and arrange for those funds to be released for this project."

"Just make sure we take the establishment with us on this," Paul told him. "We don't want God being dismissed as a crank or a stage magician. People claiming to be the new Messiah get a rough time of it. Look at David Icke."

"And why England?" asked Peter. "I thought that being an American, you'd favour the States."

"It's all down to credibility. I know what sort of an image my country has. People think that any religion that comes out of the States is based either on bible-thumping, a crank theory or a cult. But if the Good News comes out of the UK, people are gonna take it seriously. And now God's agreed to make His appearance at

Earls Court, on Christmas Day." Hiram sat back, smiling, waiting for his announcement to sink in.

The saints looked at each other. It sounded pretty tacky, but if God was willing, they could hardly criticise the plan.

"There's something else I'm not happy about," said Peter. "Sending questionnaires to our citizens. If you ask me, you're just encouraging people to be dissatisfied."

Hiram shook his head. "The dissatisfaction was already here, I'm afraid. Have you seen these?" A thick pile of papers appeared on the table. "They're petitions, letters of complaint. Look at these, for example." He handed round the petitions from the Society for the Promotion of Rights for the Remarried. "There seems to be a lot of people complaining about this particular rule. Why don't we let them live with who they like?"

"With respect, we didn't have these problems until you came along." said Paul.

"Get out of town! You'd messed up already before I arrived, That's why you wanted me on board. This rule's been there a heck of a long time, it's just that nobody's complained before. All I've done is given the people a framework for having their say, and in this case, they've got a point."

"You've got a somewhat naive view of this, if you don't mind my saying," said Paul. "If you don't impose some sort of morality on them, well, it's the thin end of the wedge. If we allow polygamy, they'll soon be having group sex, fighting amongst themselves. If they want that sort of thing, they should go to the other place."

"Let's get a perspective on this," said Hiram. "We're talking about people who've stood up and made their vows in front of the preacher."

"I agree," said Luke. "Besides, they spend their Earthly life being told what they can and can't do, why not give them a bit of freedom once they're here?"

"We have to have rules, Luke, whatever you woolly-minded

122

liberals think," said Paul. "If we let standards slip, it'll be all Hell let loose."

"There's no point in arguing about this now," said Peter, "Let's wait and see what this survey of Hiram's reveals. It may be that we'll have to look at the whole question of relationships then."

CHAPTER 8

Satan surveyed the hordes of demons and humans standing before him. It was an idea he'd picked up from Heaven; the public meeting. He liked the idea of having all his loyal subjects there at once, hanging on every word he said. Even the faithful Beelzebub was there, lying in a portable hospital bed, attached to a drip, watched over by his hawk-eyed demon nurse.

Satan cleared his throat and tapped the microphone. It gave a satisfying buzz. "My friends, you may wonder why I have gathered you all together here." His magnetic gaze swept across the monstrous hall, drawing all eyes to his. "We are about to face a momentous challenge, and we will need all our powers in order to triumph. We have been waiting for this opportunity for centuries. It is," he paused, "the Second Coming." A gasp rose from the audience. The Devil continued. "Most of you know, we denizens of Hell are barred from Heaven. Cruelly and unfairly evicted. So the only place where we can meet God and engage in battle is on Earth. Gird your loins, my faithful friends, because that battle is nigh." He picked the microphone from the stand and swept dramatically backwards and forwards across the front of the stage, addressing different sections of the crowd. "I will need you, I will need you all. We have much preparation to make. God is putting in an appearance on Earth, on Christmas Day at Earls Court. We are going to upstage Him, put on our own show that will blow Him right off stage. Everything He does, we are going to do bigger and better. It's a last-ditch attempt

124

by a clapped-out deity. He'll be left looking out over an empty auditorium. Auditions start immediately. We're on our way to Wembley."

* * *

Judas was still standing where the Devil had left him, in Julia's office. It wasn't that he was unable to move, but rather that he was waiting for his master's voice. After using Judas's eyes to scrutinise Hiram's plans, Satan had withdrawn suddenly and unceremoniously from his mind, without so much as a "bye-bye" or a "see you later". Judas was puzzled and worried about what could have happened to his new-found friend, who'd given a new purpose and meaning to his life. So he stood, and he waited, and he waited.

Then, he felt a hand on his shoulder.

"Well, well, what do we have here?" said the owner of the hand. "It's a good job that I decided to call back. I had an idea I'd find something. Don't think you can hide under all that hair and dirt, Martin Davis." Gloria held the tramp by the scruff of his neck, at arms' length. "Get a move on, you're coming home with me now." She dragged him away, struggling and protesting. His mind screamed out for his master, but there was no answer. Judas didn't know it, but his master had more important things to think about now.

* * *

"How long do you expect to be away?" asked Julia, as she helped Hiram gather his papers together.

"Just a week, in Earth time. While I'm in meetings and arranging the show, the angels will be giving away freebies to publicise the event, although we won't be releasing all the details at this stage. We're going to raise public awareness, get 'em thinking about the concept of God and Heaven. I'll be taking my mobile with me, so if you need me, just call."

"While you're gone, I'll get on with collating the results of the two surveys."

"Great, we'll need those for the next stage of the promotion. I want God to have the greatest reception He's ever had, so we gotta make people really wanna come by promising them what they want."

* * *

The doorbell rang. Lucy opened the door.

"Here you are," Gloria announced proudly, "I found him hiding in her office." She pushed the struggling tramp into the hallway, keeping a firm grip on the scruff of his neck.

"That's not my Martin!" Lucy wrinkled her nose in disgust.

"You wouldn't think so, would you? It's a brilliant disguise. You wait till we get him cleaned up and de-fuzzed, he'll be as good as new." With that, Gloria frogmarched the still-protesting vagrant up the stairs to the bathroom.

* * *

"There they go again," said the Devil, as he watched the coaches cruise through the skies. He turned to Beelzebub, who sat in a wheelchair. He was still looking peaky.

"I'm sorry, your Lowness," croaked the demon, "I'm sure I'll be as right as rain in another couple of days."

"Never mind," said Satan, "I fancy a trip to Earth myself, anyway. I'll have to leave you to hold the fort here. Manage that, can you?"

Beelzebub nodded miserably.

"I'd better be off then. I'm taking young Jake and a couple of the others with me. I'm very impressed with Jake, there's a lot of potential there – should a vacancy arise." He smiled sweetly at

Beelzebub, with just the hint of a raised eyebrow, before fastening his cape and sweeping out of the room.

* * *

Sitting on the first coach in the convoy, Tracey could hardly contain her excitement; she was returning to Earth, and this time for a whole week. She was going to make the most of it – perhaps she might see that young man again.

As the coaches drew nearer to Earth, Hiram again experienced the sensation that something was tugging at him. The feeling became stronger the closer they got to their destination, although Hiram could not give shape to its source. There was a faint inkling, a stirring of memory that brought a surreptitious tear to his eye, but it was buried too deep. He tried to relax, sure that whatever it was would come back to him eventually.

Again, the coaches diverged and headed towards their various destinations. Again, the black limousine "EVIL 1" followed Hiram's coach to a car park in London. From their parking space a few yards away, the Devil and his demons watched as the angels tumbled eagerly from the coach.

"I'll follow Hiram," said the Devil, "and Damien can come with me. Jake, I want you to see what the angels are up to. Take Mephistopheles with you."

"Can't I come with you, darling?" purred Mephistopheles.

"No you can't, you're far too . . ." He suddenly stopped in his tracks. "What the Hell are you wearing?"

"Just a little leather basque with matching tutu." He pouted. "Why, don't you like it? You usually like this sort of . . ."

"Shut up," Satan snapped. "And change into something less ostentatious. I want you to be able to blend into your surroundings. This is London, not San Francisco."

Mephistopheles sulkily transformed his clothes into a black suit with just the hint of glitter round the collar and a red satin handkerchief in the breast pocket.

"I suppose that'll have to do," said the Devil. "Now, don't forget, make sure that you don't arouse any suspicions. You've all got your mobiles?" The demons nodded. "Right, I'll ring you to arrange a meeting soon, but if any of you run into difficulties, get in touch immediately."

The four dark-suited figures left the limousine and paired off to follow their quarries. To passers-by they looked like respectable young businessmen, for their horns, tails and fangs were carefully concealed.

* * *

"We've had a serious complaint against you, your G.A.'s licence could be on the line." The Archangel Michael spoke sternly to the angel who stood to attention in front of him. Raphael was also there in his capacity as Director of Personnel, because this was a disciplinary hearing, a serious matter. "You'll no doubt guess who it's from."

"Lucy Davis?"

"Yes, Gloria. What on Earth possessed you to try to pass off a smelly tramp as that poor woman's husband?"

"It was a genuine mistake, sir. I jumped to the wrong conclusion." Gloria shrugged her shoulders. "It could've happened to anyone."

"It seems to me, Gloria, that you were perhaps a little too eager to be released from this job, so you were careless, took short cuts."

"I suppose so, sir." Gloria hung her head in shame.

"And it could have been a lot worse, but, luckily for you, the tramp didn't want to file a complaint. He would have had a good case, it was wrongful arrest." The Archangel Michael leant back in his chair. "I ought to throw the book at you."

"Yes, sir," said Gloria, who was secretly hoping that he would revoke her licence and send her to do some quiet, boring little desk job.

"But I'm not going to do that, Gloria." It was as if he had read her thoughts. "I think the most appropriate penance is to put you back on that job until you come up with a result, however long that takes."

* * *

Pamella stood in front of her full-length mirror and let the silk robe slip slowly down her smooth body. She turned to the right slowly, then to the left. She was pleased with what she saw. Everything that should be tight was tight, everything that should be pert was pert. Pert little nose, ass and tits, nipples you could hang your coat from. This body had cost thousands of dollars and had been worth every last cent. She couldn't have waited any longer, another year or two and it would have been too late; once she'd turned into a hag, there'd have been no going back.

She'd changed a lot over the past few months, from dowdy little Pammy Toogood with the frizzy brunette perm and the dresses buttoned up to the neck, transformed, like the proverbial ugly duckling, into Pamella Stepford Dietrichson, with a tautly-sculptured body and sleek blonde hair piled up on top of her head. Her own mother wouldn't recognise her now, and Hiram certainly wouldn't. She could never understand why he had liked her to look that way. "Don't ever get too skinny," he used to say. Pamella smiled into the mirror. Hiram would have been horrified at the idea of her going under the surgeon's knife, he hadn't even liked her perming her hair. "If it ain't broke, don't fix it. You're beautiful now, as God made you," he would say. Angrily, she wiped away the tear which had snuck into the corner of her eye. Stupid, stubborn man. He would have let her grow fat, saggy and wrinkled rather than let her spend more than a few dollars on her appearance. Well, she had it all now, and she could do exactly what she liked. She need never grow old, ever.

She looked over to the bed where one of her other assets lay asleep. Folks would never believe the real reason she wanted Abe. Twenty-nine to her forty-two, tanned and gorgeous, Abe's main attraction was his brain. He was a financial and legal wizard, who held the magic key that had unlocked a fortune, the fortune that should have automatically become hers by right. As she looked at him, he woke, smiled and demanded that she come back to bed. She walked towards him, thinking how damn lucky she was. But then, so was he.

* * *

The coach drew into the car park of the Paradise Cultural Complex and fifty-two Japanese businessmen piled out. Chattering with delight, they headed towards their favourite nitespot. The driver sighed. Was falling into a drunken sleep at the wheel such a crime that this was to be his punishment – a non-stop "if this is Tuesday, this must be Heaven" tour of the three dominions, which lasted for eternity and which ended up, every night, in the drink-sodden depths of Valhalla?

* * *

The meeting was held in the palace of the Archbishop of Canterbury – she was a lovely lady, thought Hiram. He wasn't so sure about the other honoured guest. Flown in under a veil of secrecy, the new Pope sat, stony-faced, surrounded by sinister looking men in dark suits and sunglasses, who had a tendency to reach suddenly inside their jackets at the slightest noise. Elected only a few weeks ago, the Pope had already been discreetly nicknamed "Don Corleone" by many of the cardinals. It was thought to be no coincidence that he'd taken the name Alexander, the same as the notorious Borgia pope.

"If what you say is true," said Alexander X in his thick Sicilian accent, "we at the Vatican want a piece of the action."

The Archbishop of Westminster looked on in alarm. As head of the Catholic Church only in England and Wales, he'd had no choice but to advise the Pope of the strange and wonderful things that had happened recently. He wasn't happy about it, but the faith taught that the Pope was infallible and he had to accept that. Besides, this wasn't the first time that the wrong person had occupied the Papal seat. Circumstances surrounding the recent Papal election had been extremely suspect, to say the least, and it was strongly rumoured that external, but not Godly, influences had interfered in the ballot. The word was that there were a couple of cardinals currently wearing concrete cassocks at the bottom of the river Tiber. The Archbishop shivered as an icy draught caressed the back of his neck; he had the feeling that he was in the presence of a great evil.

The Great Evil and Damien glided invisibly past and took up a position near the new Pope. They felt comfortable there.

"We can put money in," continued Alexander X, "but what sort of return can we expect? What are you going to charge for admission?"

"That wasn't the idea. In fact, we don't intend to charge at all. Admission will have to be decided by some sort of free lottery," said Hiram, somewhat distracted by the Archbishop of Canterbury's legs. They were the shapeliest legs that he'd ever seen belonging to a Primate of All England.

"You mean, you want us just to give you the money and get nothing back? That does not make good business sense, my friend."

"But why else have the churches been stockpiling a fortune if not for the glory of God? Surely this is what you've been waiting for?"

"You're a little naive, my friend." Alexander X paused to light his cigar. "We start giving away our money left, right and centre and suddenly, no-one will have respect for us any more. In this world, money is power."

"If you want to look at it that way," said the Archbishop of Canterbury, "don't forget that this event should prove once and for all the existence of God. After that, just watch the money come pouring in as people try to secure their place in Heaven."

"You have a point there, beautiful lady." The Pope blew her a kiss. "I tell you what, Mr Toogood, you come up with the costings and fifty per cent of the funding, and, if we're happy with your proposals, we'll put twenty-five per cent in."

"And you can count on us for the other quarter," the lady Archbishop chipped in.

* * *

Hiram had hardly been gone two flaps of an angel's wing when the problems started for Julia. First it was the newly-formed legal section. They couldn't possibly cope, they claimed, with the increasing level of work. They needed more staff, more resources, they ought to be a fully-fledged department with their own director. Every stone they turned over, something nasty would run out. Take the housing situation, for example. There were all these billions of houses, but where were the deeds, where were the tenancy agreements? Who was responsible for repairs? It was all a bodge job, and when the writs, the eviction notices and the injunctions started rolling in, how did the Trust expect the lawyers to cope, given their current staffing structure? At the moment, most of them were under extreme pressure, dealing with the complex claim submitted by a chapter of Hell's Angels.

Then there was the hospital. Julia was besieged by a deputation of nurses and doctors. "We're understaffed," they said, "and to be honest, most of us are totally unqualified. It's not pretend anymore. We're getting genuinely sick people coming in. We need professional doctors and nurses, more beds, effective drugs. There's this man called Job, he's got the worst case of boils we've ever seen and there's nothing we can do for him."

All Julia could do was to ask them to be patient for a while, until Hiram returned. She didn't want to have to call him back, his work was important and, besides, she wanted to prove that she could cope on her own.

* * *

Tracey had been sent to Euston station, and this time she was on her own. All she had to do was to hand out freebies to passers-by. It was easy. As soon as people came within a few feet of her, they would slow down, smile, and willingly accept her gifts. She couldn't understand why people weren't like that with the others: the ladies who rattled collecting tins, shabby tramps who held out their hands, people selling goods from suitcases; these were all brusquely avoided or ignored. From time to time the police would approach and most of the hawkers and beggars would hurriedly pack up and slip away; the officers would check that the ladies with the collecting tins had permits, but they didn't bother Tracey.

It was almost too easy, and after a few hours, when the novelty had worn off, Tracey let her attention wander. She thought back to the previous trip to Earth, the young man; she didn't know his name, but a vague impression of his face started to emerge in her mind. He had dark hair, she seemed to remember, and a sort of lazy smile, rather like . . .

Something in the pit of her stomach seemed to lurch. She had just seen a face, his face, if her mind wasn't playing tricks on her. He was standing about thirty feet away, with another man. He was wearing a dark suit this time, not leathers, but Tracey was sure it

133

was him. As she watched, he turned and smiled. She blushed and smiled shyly back.

"So that's your little angel." Mephistopheles wrinkled his nose in disgust. "She seems to have the hots for you. She can't take her eyes off you. Why don't you go over there and find out what she's up to?"

"All right, but stop pulling faces."

Jake strolled casually over to Tracey. "Hello, again," he said. "Remember me?"

"Yes." She smiled again, then frowned. "You took one of my forms."

"Sorry about that, I couldn't resist it, I was only teasing. If it's important, I can get it back for you."

"I don't think it matters now."

"So what are you doing this time?" he asked, pointing towards Tracey's shoulder bag, which had so far produced contents many times exceeding its apparent capacity.

"We're giving away T-shirts, aftershave and compact discs. You can have one of each if you like."

Jake took the gifts that she offered. "Thanks." He caught sight of Mephistopheles jumping up and down behind Tracey. He was gesturing towards his mobile. "I'm sorry, I have to go now, I'm due at an important meeting. Will you be here all day?"

Tracey nodded.

"Great," said Jake, "Hopefully, I'll catch you later." Before Tracey understood what was happening, he kissed her swiftly on the lips and danced away to join the other man. She shut her eyes for a second and by the time she opened them again, he was nowhere to be seen. And she still didn't know his name.

CHAPTER 9

During the series of meetings that Hiram had held with represent-atives of the various Churches, the niggle continued at the back of his mind. He was sure that, if he could only relax for a while, forget about the project, he would be able to remember, but he'd been too busy. Somehow he knew that the key to accessing the fortune he'd left behind lay somewhere in that lost piece of memory.

So he did what he'd done in the old days, when he'd been alive and had needed time to think. He found an old wooden bench in a park, with a lake, and sat down to watch the ducks. After a while, an image started to form in his mind. It was blurred at first, then came into focus as a face, a woman's face, with brown hair and green eyes. She was smiling. Then came the voice, a soft southern drawl. The words were jumbled at first, meaningless, but after a few minutes they became clear. "Not tonight, Hiram, darlin'', I have one of my headaches.' With a jolt he realised who the woman was, and knew that those words were the last she had ever spoken to him.

Tears rolled down Hiram's cheeks as the memories started to tumble back. He could understand now why Heaven erased such memories; he would never have been happy if he was aware of the bliss he had left behind. Pammy – his love, his helpmate, the matching half of his soul – how she must have suffered after his death. His only consolation was his knowledge of her inner strength; she would be supported by her belief in God and her faith in the eventual reunion of husband and wife. No doubt at this very moment she would be carrying on the good work, fighting the good fight. With the support of Abe Dietrichson, the Ministry's business manager, the fortune that Hiram had left in trust to fund good works would be in safe hands.

He would go to her at once, and she would be overjoyed to see him. Even though Hiram knew he would have to return to Heaven, the brief reunion would give him the opportunity to reassure her that one day they would be together again, for eternity. And in the meantime, what was more important, they would both have the opportunity to participate in the most significant spiritual event since the life of Christ.

The Devil and two of his henchmen sat in the black limousine; Jake in the front with his boss, Mephistopheles in the back. Damien had been left behind to keep watch on Hiram.

Satan examined the freebies that Tracey had given to Jake. He passed the aftershave to Mephistopheles, who took one sniff and pronounced that it was disgusting, sickly stuff. Then Satan unfolded the T-shirt and read the message "Climb the Stairway to Heaven". He pronounced it "Pathetic," and tossed it aside. Next he picked up the compact disc:

HEAVENTEL presents
STAIRWAY TO HEAVEN: 15 Immortal Classics
featuring Stairway To Heaven – Led Zeppelin * Angel
Eyes – Roxy Music * (If Paradise Is) Half As Nice – Amen
Corner * I Say A Little Prayer – Aretha Franklin * Heaven
Is A Place On Earth – Belinda Carlisle * Angel Face –
The Glitter Band * (There Must Be An Angel) Playing
With My Heart – The Eurythmics * Heaven Help Us All –
Stevie Wonder * Save A Prayer – Duran Duran * Angel
Of The Morning – P P Arnold * God Gave Rock And Roll

To You – Argent * Angel – The Eurythmics * Pray – Take
That * God Only Knows – The Beach Boys * Show Me
Heaven – Maria McKee * Heaven Must Be Missing An
Angel – Tavares

"Is this the best they could come up with?" he said to the others.
"It's true what they say, the Devil has all the best tunes. We can do
a lot better than this." He paused, looking thoughtfully at the disc.
"You know, Jake, this last track gives me an idea. Just think what a
victory it would be for us if we could capture us an angel . . .
You're a bit of a one for the ladies, aren't you?"

"Oh, I wouldn't say that . . ."

"Don't be bashful, I've heard the way you boast to the other
demons."

"Yeah," said Mephistopheles, pulling another of his faces, "and
you should have seen him with that angel at Euston. I couldn't
believe it when he kissed her." He leered at Jake, "Looked like he
was really enjoying it."

"What do you want me to do, sir?" asked Jake, ignoring
Mephistopheles, who was making a show of sticking his fingers
down his throat and retching.

"Tempt her away, make sure she doesn't go back to her friends.
But be careful, we can only do that if she's a willing party. If you
drag her away by force, she'll be able to call upon the full might of
Heaven to save her. You have to make her want to run away with
you."

"It'll be easy," goaded Mephistopheles, "you'll just have to give
her more of those sloppy kisses." He pursed his lips and blew a
loud kiss at Jake, who stuck out his forked tongue in reply.

"That's enough, you two," snapped Satan. "This is serious. One
more thing, Jake. No funny business, for what I have in mind, we
need a virgin."

"You'll be lucky," laughed Mephistopheles. "Haven't you heard

137

what they say about angels?"

The Devil glared at him. "If you don't shut up I'll . . ." He broke off as a panting Damien flung open the car door.

"He's vanished, sir, into thin air." The demon looked frightened. "I'm really sorry."

"So you should be," said the Devil. Damien found himself sprawled on the pavement, with no idea of how he'd got there. "Oh well, we've found out enough for the time being, I can soon pick up his scent again. Damien and Mephistopheles, you come with me, we're going to do a bit of fundraising. Jake, you call me as soon as you have the angel safely – under your thumb. But remember, that's as far as it goes."

"Before you go," smirked Mephistopheles, "I think you're going to need this." He tossed the bottle of aftershave to Jake.

* * *

Gloria was sitting at a table in the reading room of the Paradise Library, working her way through the missing persons files. She'd been surprised at how many there were, and in all the cases she'd studied so far, there was a common factor, every one of the people had disappeared since God had left and they'd all complained about being forced to live with an ex-partner. Gloria looked up from the desk, too pensive to notice the crowd of chattering Japanese tourists who flitted round her, taking photographs and filming her with their camcorders. She was on to something big here, much bigger than she'd imagined. If she could solve this mystery, the career possibilities would be limitless.

* * *

He was there again, watching her, smiling. This time he was wearing the T-shirt she'd given him, tucked into tight jeans. Tracey felt her

138

face grow hot, and she tried to ignore his presence, but she found her gaze being constantly drawn to his. The rush hour was over and she no longer had the distraction of a constant stream of customers.

He sauntered over to her. "I've got something for you," he said. He withdrew a red rose from behind his back and held it out to her. She put it to her face, breathing in its sweet scent. "Would you like to come for a walk with me?" he asked.

She shook her head. "I have to stay here." Her voice was hesitant.

"No point in hanging round here, this place will be dead for hours. Come with me, I'll take you to someplace more crowded, you can get rid of that stuff all in one go."

"We're not supposed to leave our positions until midnight."

Jake put his arm round her shoulder. "Surely you're entitled to a break?"

Tracey frowned. "No-one said anything about breaks."

"That'll be because it's taken as read. They can't expect you to stand here all day without a break, your trade union would be up in arms. You do have a trade union?"

"Yes of course."

"There you are then. If you're in a trade union, you'll have proper employment rights. It's just that no-one's bothered to explain them to you. So, what do you say? I'll show you the sights, and there'll be plenty of time to get you back before midnight."

"I shouldn't," said Tracey, "I mean, I don't even know your name."

"If that's the only problem, princess, the name's Jake." He shook her hand, then raised it to his lips and kissed it softly.

"I'm Tracey." She blushed prettily.

"Come on then, Tracey, let's not waste the little time we have." Keeping hold of her hand, Jake led her out of the station.

* * *

Hiram had just arrived in the small town in Georgia where he and Pammy had spent most of their married life. He'd deliberately chosen to arrive at a point a couple of kilometres away from the house, because he wanted to walk for a while, to firm up his memories and prepare himself for the reunion.

He thought back to his last night on Earth. It was supposed to have been his big debut at the Hollywood Bowl, the opener to his evangelical tour of the States. If all had gone well, he would have followed it up with tours of Europe, Africa and Asia, no matter if it had taken every last cent. And Pammy had been behind him every step of the way. God, what a woman, what a saint she was, he reflected. Throughout his preaching career, she'd been there, supporting him, pushing him onwards and upwards to better things. Of course she wasn't perfect, she had her little weaknesses, like the occasional hankering for material possessions and pretty clothes, but he loved her all the more for that. He was only thankful that, on that last fateful night, a headache had prevented her from joining him on stage.

Hiram stopped. He had reached the driveway to his modest little ranch home. There was a realtor's board up at the entrance. He smiled sadly. Poor Pammy, obviously she couldn't bear to live there without him. He walked up the drive, hoping that she was still living there, but he was disappointed: the place was completely deserted, the garden neglected. He dematerialised through the front door and found that the place had been stripped bare of all its homely fixtures and fittings. Hiram sat cross-legged on the floor. He knew that it was too much to expect to find a forwarding address, but he had hoped for a clue of some sort, perhaps a spiritual trail, an aura or scent that would lead him to Pammy. But there was nothing, no sign that either he or she had ever lived and loved there. It was as if the house had been exorcised of their presence. Perhaps, thought Hiram, he had been naive to think that, after death, even a love as strong as theirs would leave behind some sort of tangible manifestation. He stood up slowly, realising that he would have to look for more conventional clues.

* * *

In a small copse in the grounds of Meddlesham Hall, the wind whistled through the trees and owls hooted as a carpet of mist covered the ground. Thirteen figures stood shivering and chanting in a circle in a clearing, clutching their thin white robes around them. Most of them were wishing they were somewhere else. This was all getting a bit tiresome. They'd tried everything over the years to summon the Devil: reciting the Lord's Prayer backwards, even blood sacrifice, if a Tesco's frozen chicken could be counted. They'd scoured the libraries and bookshops for black magic books, in desperation had even studied novels by Dennis Wheatley; and had eventually found, in a seedy second hand shop, what the owner described as a fifteenth century grimoire. Duncan Crucible held the battered book in his hand and started to recite the incantation that claimed to summon demons. His wife, Edith, illuminated the page with a torch.

"Sint mihi dei acherontis propitii, valeat numen triplex Jehovae, ignei areii, aquatani spiritus salvete . . ."

There was a flash, and three dark figures appeared in the centre of the circle.

"You called?" said the Devil. He grinned. It wasn't the incantation that had called him forth; it wasn't among his principles to be "summoned" by anyone; if there were summoning to do, he would do it; but this coven, reputedly the silliest in England, had a special attraction right now. They were, to the last member, extremely wealthy, and the Devil needed their money. "I've a proposition to put to you," he said, rubbing his hands briskly. "A bit chilly out here, isn't it? Why don't we go inside where it's warm and we'll have a little chat."

A little later, the Devil lounged on the leather couch, his feet resting on a matching footstool. Edith Crucible fussed around him. Was he comfortable? Did he need another cushion? Could she get him anything to eat? To drink? Her husband sat nervously on the edge of his seat. None of the magic books he had read had told him what you did with demons once you had them in your home. There were no chapters on feeding, no guides on etiquette; they didn't even tell you how you were supposed to address the Devil. He looked uneasily at Mephistopheles, who was mincing outrageously as he handed round trays of canapés to the other members of the coven. The one called Damien seemed to be no trouble, he was chatting pleasantly to Mrs De Ville about breeding dalmations.

The Devil smiled genially at Duncan and Edith. Their fussing was getting on his nerves but he would have to bear with it, at least for the time being, for he needed their co-operation. He shook his head at Edith. "I'm very comfortable, thank you. Perhaps later, a little rare fillet steak with one of your excellent burgundies?" He turned to the husband. "So Duncan, is it a deal?"

"Well, your lordship, er, eminence . . ."

The Devil held up his hand. "Please, call me Satan, I insist, we are all friends here."

"Did you hear that, Edith? I tell you, Satan, this is the proudest day of our lives."

"Yes, yes. So, the deal?"

"It's an opportunity we wouldn't want to miss, would we, Edith?"

The Devil nodded. "Good. Now to practicalities. We'll have to arrange the booking fee for Wembley and staff costs, for a start."

"Oh please, lor – er, Satan, you must allow us to pay for all this. It's the least we can do. After all, we'll have no money worries when it's over, will we?"

The Devil smiled. These Satanists were always so gullible. "No worries at all." He shook his head. "And there is something else. I rather fancy making an album."

"An album?"

"Yes, a musical compilation." He handed the Stairway to Heaven disc to Duncan. "Something much better than this. We're also going to need merchandise to promote the show, T-shirts and posters, with a full length picture of me." He tried out one of his sexy smouldering looks on Edith, who started to have one of her hot flushes. "And one more thing, I'm expecting my other demon to arrive soon with an extra special guest, I hope that won't be a problem?"

"Our house," said Duncan, "is your house. Isn't that right, Edith?"

"Oh, yes," said Edith, "it's such an honour."

"Thank you, you won't regret your hospitality, I'll make sure that you are rewarded beyond your wildest dreams. Now, I wouldn't say no to that steak you mentioned earlier."

"What a lovely man," Edith Crucible said to her husband, later that night.

"Yes, charming," he agreed. "Not at all what I'd expected. But what surprised me the most is that he wasn't the least bit interested in our souls."

"Umm, most refreshing."

* * *

Hiram wondered whether materialising through a wall counted as breaking and entry and whether, if you were dead, it was a sin. Still, he thought, it was his only option and he was about the Lord's work. He sat down at the computer and logged on. The password was easy for anyone who knew Larry Housman, the real estate agent, and how besotted he was about his dog, Homer. It was a simple database, Hiram had only to run the cursor down a list of properties until he came to Toogood Ranch, double-click on the mouse button, and it was all there. Details of the property, the asking price, the address of the vendor. Hiram wasn't too surprised to see the name and address of his trusted business manager, Abe Dietrichson. Pammy had no head for business, so it was natural for her to ask him to supervise the sale on her behalf. He was a little disappointed not to have found Pammy's new address straight away, but the delay would only be temporary, Abe would be able to tell him where to find her.

* * *

Although Jake's reputation as a womaniser was, in a limited sense of the word, deserved, it had been achieved through no real effort on his part. Under the Demon Graduate Training Programme, he had been sent down to Earth in a series of incarnations until his soul had been sufficiently blackened by evil deeds to meet Satan's stringently low standards. In each life he'd had the advantage of good looks and an easy charm and had no difficulty in attracting women. Because he'd never had to try, he had become lazy. To Jake, women were like apples. Why take the trouble to climb the tree for the choice fruit, when he could just wait around for the windfalls which, in spite of a little bruising and the odd maggot, made perfectly good eating? There had been plenty of women, from lusty country wenches to sophisticated women of the world, who'd been only too pleased to tumble into haystacks or feather beds with Jake. He had no need for sophisticated seduction techniques.

He had no doubt that, if he'd been given a free hand, the Angel Tracey would have been horizontal by now. Women – angels being no exception – were only good for one thing. It was against Jake's every instinct to keep his hands off this one, but Satan's instructions had been explicit and Jake didn't dare disobey him. It was all he could do to hide his frustration behind a series of facial expressions, set pieces that he wore like an animated mask.

Luckily for Jake, Tracey interpreted his reserved silences as a sign of sensitivity and shyness, and warmed even more to him. They had been wandering round the city centre, Tracey handing out her giveaways while Jake tried to decide where to take her. Tracey seemed quite happy with this, she loved to window shop and to watch the other people in the crowds. He wondered whether he should take her for a meal. He had to think of something that would make her forget about rejoining her fellow angels; something, besides his innate charm, that would make her want to stay with him.

He was concentrating on possible solutions when Tracey suddenly stopped in her tracks and drew in her breath.

"What's the matter?" Jake asked.

Tracey pointed towards the entrance of a small cinema, where the signs proclaimed:

LOVEFEST

A Twenty-four Hour Celebration of Favourite Romantic
Films – Classic and Modern

Gently pulling her hand out of his, Tracey darted from one film poster to another, uttering little squeals of delight. She turned to Jake, her eyes wide and pleading, her hands clasped together as if in prayer. "Could we go in? Just for a few minutes?"

Jake smiled. "If that's what you want, princess, your wish is my command."

Inside, Jake bought the tickets and then took Tracey to the confectionery kiosk where she chose chocolates, pink and white fluffy marshmallows and a large box of tissues. It wasn't something that Jake looked forward to: watching screen romances in the company of a sickly sweet angel, but at least there was a good chance that it would distract her sufficiently to forget that she, like Cinderella, was supposed to be back at the coach before the clock struck midnight.

CHAPTER 10

It had been easier than Martin expected. He'd thought about it for a while, just waiting for Gloria to leave him alone for a precious few seconds, to give him the chance to make his escape. He'd experimented at first with a small time-jump which took him a few hours into his own past. He'd watched the Martin of that time arguing petulantly with Gloria, but neither of them could see him. Then he had projected himself further back, stopping every few years to check where he was. On the first few stops, he'd found himself still in his own back garden, the only measure of time being the diminishing size of the trees and the different flower beds that he'd planted throughout the years. On some occasions, he had been able to observe, undetected, earlier versions of himself and Lucy pottering happily together in the garden. The sight was tinged with sadness.

Eventually, he arrived at a time before his own presence in Heaven, when neither his house nor those of his immediate neighbours were in existence. He was surrounded by open space as far as the eye could see. He had no way of knowing exactly where, in Earth's equivalent timescale, he was – in his excitement and panic, he'd made no attempt to count the years through which he had travelled. He could only guess that it was perhaps forty years or more.

He looked around and spotted a warm glow in the sky, which he guessed came from the centre of Heaven, and began walking over a thin carpet of mist towards it. In the distance he could hear the familiar roars of decadent pleasure from Valhalla, a place that had remained largely unchanged for centuries. Apart, that is, from the recent introduction of "Happy Hour" and the use of little paper umbrellas to decorate the drinks, an improvement much to the liking of the Viking warriors.

As Martin walked, a black 1940's sedan drew alongside him. The driver, who to Martin looked every inch the spiv with his black hair and moustache, loud suit and hat tilted to one side, leant across and opened the door on the passenger side. "Get in," he said. Martin instinctively stepped back. "Hurry up," said the man. "You stand out like a spare part at a wedding. Do you want to be sent back to where you came from?"

Martin got into the passenger seat. Before he had had a chance to reach for his seat belt, the driver pushed down on the accelerator and the car sped away.

"Who are you?" Martin asked.

"No names, no pack drill, know what I mean?" said the driver, tapping the side of his nose with his finger. "I don't need to know anything about you, you don't need to know anything about me. Believe me, it's safer all round that way. Walls have ears, haven't you heard? Don't talk, just listen, time is precious. First thing, change your clothes. Know what a demob suit looks like?" Martin nodded. "Good, try that."

Martin shut his eyes briefly and imagined himself a new suit.

"That'll do," said the driver. "This isn't a bad time period to hide in, for a short time anyway. Because of the war, there are a lot of shell-shocked young men wandering around the place. If we should get stopped, just look dazed and say nothing. I'm taking you to a safe house where you can rest for a while and get your bearings. You'll get plenty of good advice about your new lifestyle. Then I'm afraid you'll be on your own. You're a time refugee now and it's a lonely life."

Martin noticed that they had now reached a residential area, a street with rows of semi-detached houses. His companion pulled into the drive of one of them. "This is the safe house. Ma Briggs, the lady of the house, is a sympathiser. Between you and me, I think she likes having a lot of young men around to look after." He led Martin into the house. "It's all right, Ma, it's only me. I've brought a friend along."

A matronly woman with a plump, smiling face bustled out of the kitchen. "What's this, then, Harry? Another one of your stray lambs? You make him comfortable in the living room and I'll make a fresh pot of tea."

Harry showed Martin into the living room. They sat on a settee, warmed by the glow from the coal fire. After a few minutes, Ma Briggs brought in a tray of tea, sandwiches and scones.

As they ate and drank, Harry talked quietly to Martin.

"You've run away," he said, "but what you have to understand is that you've let yourself in for a whole new set of problems. Your status is like that of an illegal alien. Officially, you don't exist. You can't have a home of your own, you can't use any of the public services or facilities, and you mustn't do anything that will bring you to the attention of the angels. If you do, they'll start asking questions, and when they find out where you're from, well, the game will be up for all of us." He paused to take a bite of his sandwich and a sip of tea.

"One day, and it could be any day, the angels from the future will wise up and start searching through time for people like us. You've got to be alert and think ahead at all times. You must plan carefully before leaping to another place, another time. You must prepare, make sure you've got the right clothes, the right hairstyle, the right vocabulary. Wherever, whenever, you are, you must blend in. Stick to out of the way places, where the angels are less likely to be. Try the places where artists and writers go, where you can be different yet still be accepted, where people won't pry. Wherever you go, you can't stay too long, you've got to keep on the move. Valhalla's a good place for a temporary refuge. And don't forget, the further back you go into the past, the less efficient the authorities are, the less regulations there'll be, but at the same time you'll have to get used to a less sophisticated lifestyle." He put his cup and plate down and went to the window, parting the net curtains a fraction and looking out at a passing car. He turned back.

"It's an interesting way of living, but by no means an easy one. You have to be on your guard at all times. It's not too late, you know. If you don't relish the idea of spending eternity as a nomad and a fugitive, then you can still go back. You can say you've been for a long walk, that you wanted space to think. But you must not tell the truth. That would only put the rest of us in jeopardy. Think about it, but don't take too long."

Martin hesitated. He thought of Lucy, of Julia, of Gloria. "I'm not going back," he said, finally.

* * *

"What time is it?" asked Tracey as she surreptitiously wiped away a tear. The credits were rolling at the end of the first film. She had looked at her watch, but the glass had blackened and she could not make out any of the features of the face. It was like looking into a deep, black hole.

"It's early yet. Why, have you had enough?

"Oh no," she said, "I could never have enough of this, but I do have to get back."

"Don't think about that, not yet, anyway. And you certainly mustn't cry about it."

"It was the film. It was Ilsa, having to leave the man she loved and get on that plane, and all for duty."

"She should have stayed," said Jake, hoping that the half-light of the cinema would hide the look of contempt on his face. He was

149

not having fun, sitting here with this sickly sweet angel as she munched her way through bags of sickly sweet chocolates and cried her way through a sickly sweet film. But he knew his duty; perhaps he could find a way to turn the sentimentality of the film to his advantage. "If she really loved him, she would have stayed," he said, turning back towards her.

"Do you think so?" Tracey looked deep into his eyes, the most beautiful, if cold, eyes that she'd ever seen. "I don't know. Somehow, if she'd stayed, I think it wouldn't have been so beautiful, so noble. It would have spoiled their love."

"It was an empty gesture," said Jake. He hoped that the other films wouldn't be too noble or he would have a Hell of a job convincing her to run away with him. He watched her now, popping marshmallows into her mouth, pink, white, pink, white, undecided as to which of the little pillows she preferred. Jake wondered, idly, how angels consumed their food. Demons had an internal combustion system, whereby food was incinerated in a small yet fierce inferno in the iron pit of the stomach. It was an efficient system, with few side effects apart from the occasional heartburn and the odd whiff of sulphurous methane. He doubted whether angels digested in the same way. He imagined their stomachs full of delicate little pockets, like a honeycomb, where the food was gently but firmly squeezed into nothingness before being puffed out in sweet-scented farts. Perhaps, when Satan had finished with this angel, he would let Jake open her up and find out.

* * *

Hiram arrived in the lounge of Abe Dietrichson's luxury Manhattan penthouse and gave a long, low whistle. The room was furnished with leather chairs, silk rugs and objets d'art, simply, tastefully – and unbelievably expensively. Boy, Abe must be doing well for himself these days; this was a far cry from the humble apartment he'd rented when he worked for Hiram. In fact, it seemed so out of character for Abe, a simple, God-fearing, hard-working young man, that Hiram wondered for a brief moment whether he'd miscalculated his trajectory when aiming himself at Abe's residence.

He walked into the next room, a dimly-lit bedroom, to find a young woman standing in front of a mirror. The woman turned and shrieked. "Sorry, ma'am," said Hiram, "wrong room." As he retreated the way he had entered – through the wall – the woman screamed again and fell to the floor. Hiram wished that there was something he could do to help; he could only hope that she would put the whole thing down to a trick of the light or a waking dream.

He wondered who the woman could be. There was certainly something vaguely familiar about her, although he was sure that she wasn't the solemn little law student whom Abe had been engaged to. He heard raised voices coming from the bedroom.

"What the Hell is up with you now?"

"He was here, standing over there, looking at me."

"Who?"

"Hiram." The woman's voice was hysterical.

Hiram glided through the wall, this time in invisible-mode, puzzled by the mention of his name. He saw Abe Dietrichson standing over the woman, gripping her slim wrist in his hand and trying to pull her up from the floor. He felt angry and disappointed with Abe for this unchivalrous behaviour.

"Don't be stupid, he's dead and gone," Abe was saying.

"I saw him, I tell you!"

"You been takin' those happy pills again? Get up and come back to bed."

The woman stood up. "No, Abe, I tell you. He was standing there. I saw him as clear as I see you now." Her eyes flitted round the room.

Abe turned on the main bedroom light. For the first time, Hiram could see the woman's face clearly and he realised the dreadful truth. He watched, paralysed, as the tableau continued to unfold.

Pamella was crying now. Abe slapped her twice across the face. "You're cracking up, you stupid bitch. We can't afford for you to crack up. We've got away with it so far, I'm not gonna let you ruin it now."

"We shouldn't have done it. Hiram was right all along. There is life after death and now he's come back for retribution." She sank to her knees. "Our only hope is to pray for forgiveness. Pray with me now, please, Abe." She reached up to take hold of his hand but he pushed her away.

"What's wrong with you, woman? I thought this was what you wanted, the money, this," he gestured towards her new face, her new body, then the luxury of the room, "and all this. And I thought you wanted me. It's too late for all that remorse shit, what's done is done. We're beyond that sort of help now. I'm gonna get us both a drink and a couple of sleeping pills." He slammed the door as he left the room, leaving her rocking back and forth on the floor, weeping.

Pamella shivered violently. She had felt a strong blast of wind, just as if a train had sped past. "Hiram?" she asked shakily. There was no reply.

* * *

Jake was beginning to despair. Following Casablanca they had watched Brief Encounter, another film with an ending that had done little for his cause. At least Tracey still seemed blissfully unaware of the passage of time. Rousing himself from his boredom, he made an attempt to use the time productively, studying her reactions to the films and taking note of the scenes which appealed to her. If he could learn her likes and dislikes, he might be able to tailor-make a romance that she would not be able to resist. This really was a poor way to spend his time; there were much more interesting things he could be doing to this little angel . . .

* * *

Edith bustled round the guest bedrooms, quickly stripping the beds and replacing the sheets. She had long been in the habit of breakfasting early when there were guests in the house, leaving her time to make the beds while they took their breakfasts. It was too bad, she thought, as she'd done many times before, that one couldn't get live-in staff nowadays. For years she had had to make do with Mrs Danvers from the village, who came for a few hours three days a week, and Mr Mellors who pottered around in the grounds, rheumatism permitting. Apart from that, Edith and Duncan muddled along as best they could, but their energies were stretched to the limit whenever they had house guests, particularly as Edith was determined to maintain the myth that the house was run by a small and efficient army of servants who were never seen above stairs.

Still, looking at the state of some of these rooms, it was a good thing that they didn't have live-in staff. It was well-known that, in the good old days, if you wanted to know the latest scandal, you had only to ask the servants. And there was plenty of fuel for gossip to be had in this house. Edith gingerly pulled the torn and scorched sheets from the Devil's bed. She thought of that nice little Damien, who'd left his bed neat and tidy, with the covers turned back so nicely. On the other hand, there was Mephistopheles, with his bed so blatantly unslept in. Edith shook her head. It was a good job that there was no servant to see this. There was already too much talk in the village about strange goings on at the big house.

Feeling more than a little exhausted, Edith sat on the bed to rest for a moment. She caught sight of her reflection in the mirror. She didn't like what she saw: a dumpy little middle-aged woman, with a flushed face and short, grey, wiry hair that she could never do anything with, wearing twin-set, tweeds and sensible lace-up shoes. She had a picture in her mind of the sort of glamorous witch that she had always wanted to be: a shapely beauty with long, black hair, long, spiky, red nails and a long, black dress, which skimmed over perfect curves then flared out around her ankles. Someone like Morticia in The Addams Family or Lily in The Munsters. Try as she might, she couldn't project her own image into that of her ideal witch-goddess, but she hoped that all that would change soon. The Devil had promised Duncan and Edith the ultimate reward in return for their help and Edith knew what she would be asking for.

* * *

"What time is it now?" asked Tracey.

Jake looked at his watch. "Still early, only half-past nine," he lied, easily. He forced himself to smile at her. "I preferred that one. At least it had a happy ending. Tears along the way, but it all came right in the end."

"Have you ever been to New York, to the Empire State Building?"

"Yes," said Jake. "It was . . . breathtaking." He remembered his last visit there, in the thirties – the magnificent view as he leant over the rails and watched his one-time business partner plunge to his death. That had been two incarnations ago. Ah, happy days.

The two films with noble endings had been followed by two others where the lovers had been parted by death, Love Story and Ghost. Jake couldn't understand how Tracey could cry her eyes out and then say how much she had loved the films. The next two, An Affair to Remember and Sleepless in Seattle, had both ended happily, eventually, and Tracey had cried just as much. It was a mystery to Jake, but then he had never understood women.

As the cinema darkened and the opening titles for the next film started to roll, Jake realised that he would have to push things along a little bit faster. He moved his arm along the back of Tracey's chair and rested it lightly along the top of her wings. He felt her lean across and rest her head on his shoulder. He knew that he daren't go much farther, but she was so temptingly close.

* * *

Raphael walked down the length of the coach, counting, "Forty-two, forty-four, forty-six, forty-eight, fifty." He returned to the front and frowned. "There is definitely one missing."

"Are you sure?" asked Gabriel. "Don't forget we're one short anyway, Hiram's not back."

"Of course I haven't forgotten, I'm not stupid. There should be fifty-one, including us two, but not including Hiram. Let me have the list, we'll have to have a roll-call." Clipboard in hand, he turned to the coachload of angels. "Quiet, everyone." he said. The chattering stopped immediately. "When I call your name out, answer loud and clear. Alison?"

"Yes."

"Angus?"

"Yes."

* * *

Crisis piled upon crisis. *The Herald* reported that there had been a near-riot in Valhalla, sparked off by a clash between the resident Viking warriors, a group of Hell's Angels and a coachload of Japanese businessman. As a result, Odin had banned all outsiders from the club until further notice. Then, a group of deserted wives had marched on Eternity Hall, demanding the return of their missing husbands. They were headed by one Lucy Davis who blamed the disappearances on maladministration by the authorities. The

Japanese businessmen, whom the authorities had been seeking for some time, had also disappeared again.

The radio crackled.

"This is Earth calling Heaven, come in, Heaven. Over."

"Heaven receiving you, loud and clear. Julia Davis speaking. Identify yourself. Over."

"This is Gabriel from Coach One calling. We have a problem. One of our angels is missing."

"What do you mean, missing?" Julia frowned.

"The Angel Tracey has not returned to the coach. We have checked her last known whereabouts, but there is no trace, no Tracey." He laughed, pleased with his little joke.

Julia drew a sharp breath before replying. "Very funny, in the circumstances. Is Hiram there?"

"No, although we weren't expecting him back yet. The trouble is, we've tried to contact him on his mobile but there's no reply."

Julia pushed her hair back from her forehead. "What can I do to help?"

"I hoped that you'd be able to tell me that. You're the one who's supposed to be in control of things up there."

Julia could picture the expression of sarcasm on his face.

"I would have thought," she said, slowly, "that you'd be better placed than me to conduct a search. You are a bit closer, after all."

"Yes, but we haven't got access to all those Heavenly powers. I suggest that you call in the saints. You're out of your depth, lady."

"Leave me to handle things up here. You concentrate on a full search of the area." Her voice was crisp and firm. "Someone had better stay near the radio in case she comes back or I need to contact you again. In the meantime, I'll keep trying to get through to Hiram. Over and out.

"Damn, damn, damn," she muttered to herself. There was no way that she was going to go running to the Trustees, admitting that she couldn't cope. She was sure that it would be the last thing

156

that Hiram would want her to do. She picked up the 'phone and dialled Hiram's number.

"I'm sorry," announced a female voice in clipped tones, "the number you are calling is not available at present. Please try later."

CHAPTER 11

The lights in the auditorium came up and stayed up as the audience filed out, most of them dabbing at their eyes with soggy tissues. Tracey stayed fixed in her seat, staring at the screen.

"That was wonderful," she sighed.

"If you like," said Jake, "we can watch them all over again." He wasn't sure that she was under his spell yet. He needed more time, to let her steep for a little longer in romance. If he moved in too early, he could ruin everything.

"No, I have to get back." Tracey looked at him suddenly, panic in her eyes. "What time is it? We must have been in here for hours." She jumped to her feet and turned round to look at the clock on the wall. Jake prepared for her outburst. She sat down again. "It's all right, it's only half-past eight." She frowned. "But it was nearly nine o'clock when we came in." She looked at Jake. "Oh God! It must be half-past eight in the morning, I'm dreadfully late."

"No way," said Jake. "It's still night, I'm sure. Come and look outside." He led her out of the cinema. "See how dark it is? That clock has probably stopped."

"Oh, yes," she said. "It's magical, we've seen all those films, I thought that we must have been here for hours. I didn't think that time was like that here. It's just like it is in . . ." She stopped, realising that she had been close to giving away the secret of who she was and where she'd come from.

"Well?" asked Jake. "Would you like to see them again, or shall we go somewhere else?"

"I wouldn't mind watching just a couple more, if you don't mind," she said, shyly.

He smiled. "Whatever you want, princess." It had been absurdly easy. She was so stupid, not realising that the reason why it was dark outside was that she had sat through twenty-four hours worth of films. If necessary, he could keep her there for days on end. He paid for another twenty-four hours worth and then took Tracey back into the cinema.

"I forgot to buy more chocolate," he said suddenly. "Wait here while I fetch some, I won't be long."

He returned to the kiosk in the foyer and bought more sweets, then went to a quiet corner, took his mobile from his jacket pocket and tapped the buttons.

"I was beginning to think that we'd lost you," said Satan. "What have you been up to? I hope you've kept our little angel – safe."

"No problem, boss. She's safe as houses here. We're just watching a film or two, getting to know each other, you know."

"Well just make sure you keep your hands off, no hanky panky – she's mine, remember. Are you going to bring her here when you're ready?"

"I think it might be better if she doesn't know I'm with you, at least for the time being. Is there somewhere we could hide away?"

"I'm sure we can find something suitable, a nice little cockroach infested hovel, perhaps?"

"I was thinking more along the lines of a quaint little cottage with roses round the door. And it might help if we fill the place with the kind of stuff she likes so much, chocolates, flowers, slushy love songs and videos of romantic films – nothing too raunchy though."

"All right, I'll make the necessary arrangements. Let me know when you're ready to move and I'll tell you how to get there."

Jake returned to the cinema and slipped back into his seat just as the film was about to start. He wasn't sure what was worse, the wrath of Satan, if he should fail, or the derision of his fellow demons when they found out, as they surely would, that he had missed out on corrupting this angel. It would be the end of his reputation as a ladykiller. But there was no way out, he had to learn new skills for this situation, and quickly. He had already built up a picture of her likes and dislikes. She seemed to prefer the older films, the classic black and whites, with their noble sacrifices and the lovers separated by tragedy. She flinched at the strong language and relatively explicit sex scenes of the modern films; but, on the other hand, she seemed to like the happy endings. He decided that their artificial love story would be one of star-crossed lovers and he would make her believe that there would be a happy ending. He was sure that he would be able to sustain her romantic dreams on a diet of hand-holding, lingering looks and a few chaste kisses, which was all he was allowed.

Outside the dark auditorium, in the foyer of the cinema, the cashier opened the drawer of her cash register. "Bloody Hell, Elsie, there's slime everywhere – just like last time."

Elsie, behind the counter of the refreshment kiosk, opened her till. "Same here, Cynth. Do you suppose there's something wrong with the tills?"

"No, if you ask me, it's someone's idea of a practical joke." Cynthia dabbed at the stinking mess with a tissue. "Just wait till I get my hands on whoever has done this."

Outside, in the streets of London, the angelic search party was still combing the streets. They carried photographs of Tracey and stopped passers-by, asking them if they'd seen her. But it was a hopeless search: there were so many angels around these days, the people said, and they all looked the same. The Angel Heather walked past the cinema twice. It never occurred to her to look inside.

* * *

160

THE NINE O'CLOCK NEWS

"Police investigating the missing Eurotrek coach linked with the recent motorcycle crash on the M1 have been inundated with reports of sightings from all over the British Isles. Several reports have apparently placed the coach at cities as far apart as Glasgow, Stoke-on-Trent and Exeter almost simultaneously. Psychologists have suggested that these claims may have arisen from an unusual manifestation of mass hysteria. Police are reported to be re-examining film from motorway surveillance cameras . . ."

* * *

Julia paced the floor of her office. For hours, she'd been trying to reach Hiram through his mobile, but there had been no response. According to Gabriel, the little angel was still missing. Julia felt guilty about that; after all, she'd been the one who'd persuaded Hiram to take Tracey down to Earth in the first place. She would never forgive herself if anything happened to the angel just because she was too proud to ask the saints for help. Julia stopped walking. She had an idea. There was one saint whom she could trust. Picking up the 'phone, she dialled Maggie's number.

* * *

Pammy looked at her reflection in the mirror. All the pain, all the expense, it had all been for nothing. In one night, the fifteen years she'd shed had reclaimed her. Her jaw hung slack, her cheeks sagged, her hair hung lank around her face. It was as if she'd been held together by tiny, invisible stitches, which had suddenly been unravelled. At least Abe hadn't seen her like that. He'd got up early and left the apartment while she lay, half-awake, telling her that she'd better pull herself together before he got back in the evening.

Pammy looked in the mirror again then wailed, wringing her hands, and cried out to God to help her.

God didn't hear her. His attention was elsewhere, on Ant World, where Armageddon was close at hand. The two most powerful ant nations each had their thermonuclear warheads aimed at each other, and the two leaders had their antennae poised over the firing buttons.

But Pammy's cries did not go unheard. There was a being who had developed an ear for the sound of souls in torment, for voices crying in the wilderness. And at this moment he was only a few thousand miles away, across the Atlantic.

Satan's ears pricked up, but he finished off his slice of seedcake and drank his cup of tea before turning to Edith.

"Thank you," he said, "that was very nice. Now, if you'll excuse me for a few hours, I have some business to attend to."

As he rose, Mephistopheles and Damien also stood. The Devil waved them down. "No," he said, "you two stay here, I won't be long. Besides, you can make yourselves useful, help Mrs Crucible get the cottage ready." The Devil had explained the need for a place where the young lovers, who would arrive soon, could be alone together; and Duncan and Edith had agreed to make a small cottage in the grounds of their estate available. Satan brushed the crumbs from his trousers, then vanished in a puff of sulphurous smoke.

* * *

Saint Paul knocked on the front door, but there was no answer. Letting himself in through the side gate, he went into the back garden. Saint Peter was there, tending his rockery. He looked up as Paul walked down the path.

162

"Seeing as I've been put out to grass, I thought I might as well do a bit of gardening."

"I shouldn't worry, they'll be needing us soon enough. I've heard rumours things aren't going too well."

"If you're talking about Hiram and a missing angel, I've heard about that. I may be old, Paul, but not much gets past me. Pass me that trowel, would you."

Paul handed over the tool. "So what are we going to do about it? Surely now is the time for us to take charge again?"

"Where's the hurry?" Peter looked up at Paul then started to attack a particularly stubborn weed with his trowel. "What do we have so far? Two missing persons; one, an insignificant angel, the other, a pain in the neck. We can afford to let matters get a lot worse before we charge in, cavalry-fashion, to the rescue."

* * *

Martin had found his refuge, somewhere he could stop to refuel in between his forays through time. It was a place where his presence was accepted without question.

He had been fascinated by the way in which Heaven had reflected the popular cultures of Earth through the ages. It seemed that many of the citizens of Heaven had always been more than ready to try out the new ideas and fashions which the newly deceased brought with them. At the same time, there were those who clung to the old ways. Martin had noticed that the evolution of Heaven could be traced through the geography of its streets, their layout and architecture, which could be read like the rings of a tree-trunk. The older parts of Heaven were at the centre, and as Heaven had expanded outwards throughout the centuries to accommodate new citizens, the different architectural styles and cultural features had formed into roughly concentric circles around the core. Martin had made a study of this development, it was his way of bringing purpose to his nomadic wanderings.

His favourite place had first come into existence during the late nineteenth century, when the great French impressionist painters had slowly gathered together to recreate Montmartre. Manet had arrived first in 1883, but it had taken over forty years, in Earth time, for the circle to be completed. Here, Martin loved to sit at the pavement tables outside the cafes and sip absinthe as he listened to Manet, Monet, Degas and Renoir, amongst others, expound their philosophies of life, love and art. Moving backwards and forwards in time, he often turned up to recapture the experience of their emotive reunions, to see them embrace one of their newly deceased friends and to join in the celebrations. Martin had never before felt such a sense of complete belonging. He told himself that he'd always had artistic leanings; that, with the slightest encouragement, he could have produced great works of art. Instead, he told himself, he'd been pushed along the traditional middle class path of career and domesticity. But it was not too late. After all, this was Heaven and Martin had all the time in the world to learn; so, as he continued his sight-seeing tour through time, he got into the habit of carrying a sketchpad with which to record his observations. But he never showed this to anybody, least of all his artist friends.

One of Martin's most treasured possessions was a small sketch that Degas had made of him sitting outside the cafe. This was something that happened frequently: one of the artists, suddenly inspired by the feeling of a particular moment, would set up his easel and record the scene for posterity. Martin felt honoured to have been present at the birth of such great masterpieces, and especially to have been pictured in some of them.

In his travels, Martin occasionally encountered other fugitives. There was no mistaking them, it was as if they emitted secret signals only recognised by fellow travellers. When this happened, the individuals concerned would simply nod briefly at each other, then turn off in their separate directions.

* * *

The longer he watched the films, the more time Jake had to rehearse his performance. He studied and then practised the expressions on the faces of the actors; in Brief Encounter, the way Laura looked when she first realised that she loved Alec; and, when they were sitting at a table in the railway station buffet, the way he droned on about lung diseases and she just looked totally absorbed in his hands. During Casablanca, An Affair to Remember and Love Story, he studied the way that Rick and Ilsa, Ricki and Terri, and Oliver and Jennifer gazed in adoration at each other.

He also listened attentively to the words and their delivery, until he was able to memorise whole scenes. He was confident that he would later be able to quote them word for word, to adapt them according to his needs, or even to invent his own false sentiments. He smirked unseen in the dark cinema. Perhaps he had missed his vocation in past lives. With a talent like his, he could have been up there on that silver screen with all the other hams.

* * *

Pammy watched impassively as the figure slowly materialised in the corner of the room like the image in a Polaroid.

"Hiram?" she asked tentatively, but it was soon obvious to her that it wasn't him.

"You went to a Hell of a lot of trouble to rid yourself of him," said the figure, "surely you don't want him back now?"

She looked at him. He was stunning. He had to be the most beautiful man she could ever imagine. "Who are you?" she asked.

"A friend," said the Devil.

165

She stared into his dark eyes, fathoms deep. "Are you some sort of angel?"

"Hardly, but you're getting warm." Satan smiled. "Let's just say that I'm from the other side."

Pammy was still unsure. "Did Hiram send you?"

"No, you did. You called out, remember?"

Pammy paused. She could only remember calling out for . . . "God?"

The Devil laughed. "I should forget about God and Hiram if I were you. You've definitely burnt your boats as far as they're concerned. Hiram's pretty powerful up in Heaven and he's not going to let his murderer anywhere near the place. If you want to make a bid for Heaven you're going to have to be prepared to wear sackcloth and ashes for a very long time." He smiled and moved nearer. "Your best bet would be to throw in your lot with us. I don't think you were ever cut out for sainthood, Pamella. I know what makes you tick."

As he moved nearer, Pammy found herself growing hot; her breathing became quick and shallow as she breathed in the hot musky air. Every inch of her body tingled. One touch and she knew she would dissolve.

The Devil turned as he heard a noise outside. The bedroom door opened and Abe walked in. He looked at Pammy, standing there, her lips parted, her pupils dilated. She was dressed only in her robe. Abe looked from her to the man standing near her. "Up to your old tricks again, darlin'? I suppose I was flattering myself to think that you wouldn't double-cross me the way you did Hiram. God, you look just like a bitch on heat." He walked towards her, his hand raised ready for the strike.

"God," said the Devil, "has nothing to do with it." His eyes flashed and Abe Dietrichson was suddenly a column of flame, which quickly reduced to a small pile of ashes. Pammy screamed.

"Forget him," said the Devil. "He was just small-fry. You were

166

already getting tired of him. There's nothing doing for you here anymore. Come, I will show you pleasures you could never imagine." He held out his hand and Pammy, mesmerised, walked slowly towards him. The Devil smiled. Now he had a valuable hostage, an insurance policy in case Jake should fail with the angel.

* * *

"I'm glad you called me," said Maggie. She was sitting opposite Julia in the Ambrosia Cafe.

"I just didn't know what to do for the best," said Julia. "I knew I couldn't handle it all by myself, but I didn't want to go to the other Trustees, not behind Hiram's back. But I know that you're his friend and I can trust you."

"You've done the right thing," soothed Maggie. "There's nothing the Trustees can do that we can't do just as well, if not better, if we put our heads together. This is our chance to prove ourselves. Let's list the problems."

"Right," said Julia, "Tracey's missing, God knows where. I can't contact Hiram and I haven't got a clue about how far he's got with this Second Coming. Complaints about the services in Heaven are flooding in, my husband's disappeared and I'm being hounded by his first wife and his guardian angel. That about sums it up."

"Right," said Maggie. "We can forget about the complaints up here for the time being. We have to give priority to what's happening on Earth. These disappearances are ominous. Angels don't just go missing, someone must have lured this one away. I suspect that the Forces of Evil are behind this, and possibly behind Hiram's disappearance, too, although I would have thought that he could look after himself. If conventional methods have failed to make contact, we'll have try alternatives." She paused. "Have you ever heard of The Red Indian Club?"

"Yes," said Julia. She remembered seeing the poster once in the reception of Eternity Hall. It hadn't been there on other visits.

"It's a secret organisation," said Maggie. "Officially it doesn't exist, but unofficially the authorities turn a blind eye to its activities, as long as it remains harmless and the numbers involved don't get out of hand."

"What does it do?"

"Its members communicate with people on Earth. Usually, they're people who have resisted the amnesiac effects of Heaven and who try and stay in contact with their loved ones. There are others who do it as a hobby. Saints and angels are barred, so I can't join. But they might let you in."

"Where do I find it?"

"Oh they'll find you. It'll probably be when you're least expecting it, but that's how they operate, for security reasons."

* * *

The cinema lights went up. Jake and Tracey had sat through another twenty-four hours worth of films. Jake swallowed. They were all there in his head, the corny lines, the loving expressions, the dramatic gestures. Now was the time for him to give the performance of his life. He turned to Tracey and looked deep into her eyes.

"Thank you for the most wonderful day of my life."

Tracey blushed and looked round nervously. The cinema was now empty. She looked up at the clock on the wall. Again it said half past eight. She remembered that Jake had said that it was broken, but that couldn't be true, she could see the second hand moving round. An usher was walking down the aisle towards them.

"Excuse me, is that clock right?" she asked.

"Never wrong, that clock," said the usher. "Regular as clockwork, to use the proverbial. Now, unless you two lovebirds are going to buy another day's worth of tickets, I'm afraid you'll have to leave. It's nearly time for the next showing."

168

Tracey turned to Jake, a puzzled look on her face. "What does he mean, another day?"

"I'll explain later," he muttered.

Tracey turned back to the usher. "How long have we been in here?"

"Two days, of course." He looked from Tracey's panic-stricken face to Jake. "What's going on here? Do you want me to fetch a policeman, miss?"

"No," she said, "but I must go now." She sprang out of her seat and ran up the aisle.

Jake followed her. "Wait, there's something I have to say to you."

But she carried on, and Jake had no choice but to follow her. He had to think quickly. Once out of the cinema, Tracey stopped. "Which way to the coach?" she asked.

"I don't know," said Jake. Tracey had no way of knowing that he was lying, that he'd followed her from the coach to the station in the first place. She bit her bottom lip and thought for a few seconds.

"I'll have to go back to the station and find my way from there." She started to walk briskly towards the railway station. Jake caught up with her; he knew he had to come up with something pretty impressive, and soon. Throughout his many incarnations and innumerable sexual conquests, he had prided himself on never having had to utter those three little words, but this situation called for the ultimate sacrifice. He pictured the actors in the films and imagined himself in front of the camera. "Don't you realise that I've fallen head over heels in love with you?"

Tracey stopped, blushed and giggled nervously. This was not how she was supposed to behave, she knew that. Neither Celia Johnson nor Ingrid Bergman would giggle like a silly angel. She stopped giggling and tried to look sophisticated.

Jake continued, "I love your big, beautiful eyes, your shy smile."

Tracey shook her head. "I'm sorry, but I have to go, I'm already terribly late."

"Love means you never have to apologise," said Jake. He grasped her hand and looked at her as if he loved her.

Tracey, gently and sadly, pulled her hand away and said, "No, you don't understand. It's impossible. I don't belong here." She started to walk away.

"Please, don't be so cruel." Jake hurried to reach her.

She looked away and carried on walking, but not before he had spotted the tear forming in the corner of her eye. He had to try harder, he couldn't afford to let her slip away from him now. He would really have to lay it on thick. "It's ironic," he said, with crocodile tears in his eyes, as they approached the station.

"What is?" asked Tracey.

"It's only just occurred to me. Brief Encounter, it could almost be our story, as if we were destined to meet, to replay the film. Don't you see?" Jake gestured dramatically around him. "The railway station, the role it played in their romance, like ours, and the cinema, they used to go to the cinema together. Please, I implore you, you be Laura, I'll be Alec, but this time let's make it a happy ending. We can't miss this, our one chance of happiness. If we say goodbye now, we'll never see each other again."

"I've got no choice. I must find the others, they'll be looking for me."

Jake decided to try new tactics. He had to go for it, all or nothing. He caught hold of her arm. "You're right, there are too many obstacles to our love, neither of us is free." He sighed. "Besides, I can't expect you to trust me, you hardly know me."

"Oh please don't," said Tracey. She stopped walking and turned towards him, her eyes tearful. "It's not you, I mean, if I was just an ordinary girl, it would be different. I can't explain."

"You don't have to, I know what you are," said Jake. "I've known it from the start. It's probably what drew me to you. Like you, I'm

170

different. In fact," he looked down at the floor in mock humility, "I am not good enough for you. It's probably best that we part, I would only drag you down. Besides, it would be a disaster for us to be seen together."

"What do you mean?" asked the angel.

"I haven't told you the worst. This isn't just another 'boy loves girl' story, this is 'demon loves angel'." He saw her step back, mouth open with shock.

"That's why I couldn't tell you, I knew that you would be horrified. All I can ask is that you forgive me for falling in love with you. I didn't mean to fall in love, but we can't pretend it never happened."

"I'm not horrified, it just came as a shock. I mean, you're nothing like what I imagined a demon would be."

"I'm just an ordinary minor spirit, like you, only I took a different path. It was the wrong path, I can see that now. But it's too late. Oh, why is life so difficult?" Jake sighed, and looked up again, into her eyes. "Oh, if only I didn't love you so much."

"Perhaps, there is a way we could be together?" said Tracey, the tears trickling down her cheeks.

Jake made his eyes water in reply. He was sure that she'd taken the hook, but didn't want to lose her at this stage by being too impatient. He would throw her a few more lines before reeling her in. He shook his head. "No, it would be too difficult, we live in different worlds, it would be an enormous strain. We must part, but we must be careful, prepare ourselves, it would be cruel to our hearts if we were to part too suddenly." He put his hands on her shoulders. "I love you and I will love you for eternity. All I ask is that you promise never to forget me. Will you promise?"

"Oh yes, but does it have to be like this?"

"Let's just go and sit down together, for a few moments." Jake led her into the station and looked round desperately. What he needed, to set the scene, was an old fashioned railway station with a drab and dusty buffet and a platform only yards away. He wanted to be able to rush to the platform's edge, to stop at the last minute as the train thundered past in clouds of steam, for a last, dramatic gesture. That was what he wanted, but what he had instead was a modern station, filled with TV monitors and electronic messages, a selection of fast food kiosks and platforms half a mile away. He had to do the best he could, which was to take Tracey into a burger bar where they sat and sipped coke from plastic cups. Jake said little, just watched her, until she looked at him with that look of love, like Laura, like Ilsa. Then he stood up and said, "It's no use, I must go now." With that he strode out purposefully, into the concourse and out of the station entrance. He sensed, rather than heard, Tracey following him. Out in the road, he saw a double-decker 'bus approaching. Measuring every step, Jake ran to the edge of the pavement, coming to a dead halt at the very brink, then grinned as the 'bus swerved slightly away from him and the driver raised his fist. He heard a gasp of shock from Tracey behind him. "I'm sorry," he said, turning to her. "I stood there on the very brink, but there's no way I can leave you now."

Sobbing, she ran into his arms. "I love you very, very much," he said, "with my heart and soul." He found it so much easier to lie when he didn't have to look her in the face. "There's no reason for us to feel guilty, we know that we love each other and that's all that matters."

As Jake felt her arms tighten around him, he smiled. He'd got her, now all he had to do was get her away safely. "Come back to the burger bar and we'll make our plans," he said. "I know of a place where we can hide, I just have to make a 'phone call."

CHAPTER 12

Julia had spoken aloud the words "I want to join the Red Indian Club" several times, but nothing had happened. Perhaps she was supposed to stamp her foot or spin round three times, but she was already attracting odd looks, with people thinking she was talking to herself. She passed a large group of women, who were brandishing placards bearing the legend "First Come, First Served" as they listened to a woman who stood on a small podium. "We are at the mercy of a woman," she was saying, "who has raised herself to an elevated position here in Heaven, a woman who is serving her own interests, a woman, herself a second wife, who has stolen and hidden away my husband." It was Lucy Davis, so carried away in her rhetoric that she failed to spot that the object of her hatred was discreetly hurrying away. Julia had more important things on her mind than getting involved in a slanging match with her rival.

Julia let herself into her room, threw her jacket on the chair and kicked off her shoes before realising that somebody was in the room with her. She looked up and recognised the young follower of fashion, resplendent in black leathers and draped with chains. "Hello, Jeff. What are you doing here?"

"I've come to escort you to the Red Indian Club." He grinned at her.

Maggie had said that it would happen just when she least

expected it, and it had, just as Julia had fleetingly forgotten about the club.

"Here we are," said Jeff, as they materialised in a large, darkened room. "Sorry about all this, but non-members can only come if they're accompanied by a member."

Julia found it impossible to estimate the numbers in the room; there seemed to be a constant flow of people coming and going. They seated themselves around circular tables, which expanded or contracted as necessary, so there were never any empty spaces. Each table was almost entirely covered by a large, transparent dome. Julia followed Jeff to one of the tables and sat down in the vacant seat which appeared in front of her. No-one spoke to her, or showed any sign of being aware of her presence. She looked at the dome, sure that she had seen something move within it. When she looked closer, she realised it was a group of people, sitting around a table, holding hands, and she could hear them talking.

"Is there anybody there?" came the voice of an elderly lady from within the dome.

"What's happening?" whispered Julia to Jeff, who had taken a seat to the right of her.

"We're communicating with Earth, seance to seance," he explained. "It's easier for us, because we have no doubts up here. We know for sure that the other side exists. But down there," he nodded towards the dome, "there's always somebody who's sceptical, and it's that which makes communication so difficult. Now, hold hands and concentrate on the dome."

"Is there anybody there?" the woman asked again.

"HELLO, DORIS, THIS IS CHIEF RUNNING STITCH." Julia almost jumped out of her skin as Jeff's voice boomed out. She saw the old woman in the dome stiffen.

"My spirit guide is coming through," said Doris. "Do you have a message from the other side for anyone here today, Chief?"

"YES, ASK THE WOMAN WHO WORKS AT HARVEY NICHOLLS

174

WHAT LENGTH HEMLINES ARE GOING TO BE IN NEXT SEASON."

"I'm getting something through." Doris looked round her table. "Has anyone here had a Harvey or a Nicholas pass over to the other side?"

"Could it be Harry? My husband's name was Harry," said a thin, bespectacled woman.

"It might be, the message is very faint," said Doris. "He said something about watching the headlines, does that make any sense?"

"Not really," said the woman. "My Harry knows I never read the papers."

"Perhaps," suggested one of the other women, "perhaps he means that if you read the headlines, you might see something to your advantage?"

"Yes," said another. "Perhaps you're going to come into an inheritance."

"Let me try again." Doris squeezed her eyes tightly shut. "Are you there, Chief, can you repeat your message?"

"I WANT TO KNOW WHAT THE COLOURS ARE FOR NEXT SEASON," boomed Jeff.

"I'm getting him again," said Doris. "He's talking about someone called Arthur, is there anybody here who's lost an Arthur?" The people round the table thought hard then shook their heads.

Jeff tried again. "WHAT IS EVERYBODY WEARING?"

"Ooh, that's clearer," said Doris, "that's coming through quite strong."

"Thank God," said Jeff.

"What did he say, Doris?" asked the woman sat beside her.

"I can hardly credit it," said Doris. "He says it's Eddie Waring."

"What, him off It's a Knockout?"

"I think so."

"OH, THIS IS USELESS," Jeff shouted at the figures in the dome.

"I heard something too that time," said one of the other women round Doris's table. "He said something about my Eustace. This is a miracle, Doris."

"It's no good," said Jeff. "Let's try another table."

"I don't want to be rude," said Julia, "but I didn't come here to find out the latest fashion tips."

Jeff smiled politely. "I'm sorry, I just assumed you had taken an interest. Are you wanting to get in touch with a loved one?"

"Not exactly, but I am looking for some missing persons."

"Oh right. We'll try Harriet's table. Harriet was a medium on Earth and she's had some impressive results since she's been up here with us." Julia followed him to another table, presided over by a lady dressed like a gypsy fortune-teller in brightly coloured shawls and beads. Jeff whispered briefly to the woman, who looked impassively at Julia, then nodded. Jeff signalled to Julia to sit down.

"I'm told you're looking for missing persons," said Harriet. "Please explain, my dear. Is it someone you've left behind and are worried about?"

"No, I'm looking for three people who are missing from Heaven."

Harriet looked puzzled. "I wouldn't have thought that was possible. You'll have to tell me the full story."

Julia explained how Hiram and Tracey had disappeared while visiting Earth and how Martin had vanished into thin air in Heaven.

"Well, I dare say it's most irregular, but I'll give it a try." Harriet looked at the dome and the scene inside dissolved, to be replaced by another seance scene. "We'll try Betty. She has a powerful psychic talent which makes up for some of her other little deficiencies."

Julia looked inside the dome. The evidence of one of Betty's little deficiencies was right there, in the half full glass on the table and the half empty bottle on top of the sideboard behind her. Unlike the medium in the dome at the other table, Betty was alone.

"HELLO BETTY, HARRIET HERE." She leaned over to Julia and whispered, "I don't go in for any of that Red Indian nonsense with Betty, she's far too sharp for that."

"Hello, Harriet, you old slag." The woman in the dome raised

176

her glass and took a mouthful of the amber liquid. "What can I do for you today?"

"I'VE GOT AN UNUSUAL PROBLEM FOR YOU TODAY. WE'RE LOOKING FOR SOME LOST SOULS, PEOPLE WHO HAVE PASSED OVER TO OUR SIDE, BUT HAVE GONE MISSING."

"Well," said Betty, "if you lot up there can't trace these folks, I doubt whether I can but, what the Hell, I'll try anything once, as the actress said to the bishop."

"THERE'S SOMEONE HERE WITH ME WHO KNOWS THEM. I'LL TRY TO SET UP A PSYCHIC LINK BETWEEN YOU AND HER." Harriet gripped Julia's hand tightly. "Concentrate hard, fix a visual image of each of them in your mind, one at a time. ARE YOU READY, BETTY?"

"Go ahead." After a while, Betty opened her eyes. "That's it, I reckon I've got the picture." She accurately described the three missing people. Draining the remains of her drink, she turned the glass upside down. "I reckon the ouija board is my best bet," she said.

"Oh, dear," whispered Harriet. Jeff laughed nervously.

"What's the matter?" asked Julia.

"You'll see soon enough," said Harriet. "For the time being, just keep your fingers crossed."

They watched as the glass under Betty's finger chased back and forth, side to side, across the table, letter to letter. The glass stopped and Betty spoke. "July, a massage from dog, donut woozy."

"What does it mean?" asked Julia. "Is it in code?"

"No," laughed Harriet, "I'm afraid that it's another one of Betty's little deficiencies. She's dyslexic. We just have to work it out."

At that moment something fluttered onto the table, it was a piece of paper, a telegram, "JULIA, A MESSAGE FROM GOD – DON'T WORRY. STOP."

* * *

177

The London coach stayed on Earth for three days longer than planned. After that, Gabriel insisted that they return to Heaven. He didn't like to stay too long, it made him nervous, the young angels were so quick to pick up Earthly habits that Gabriel was worried they would all go missing. Michael was worried about leaving Tracey and Hiram stranded on Earth, so they left behind a special telephone box, which would only be visible to the two missing people and which was linked directly to Heaven.

Immediately on the angels' return, Gabriel convened a Trade Union meeting.

"Health and Safety at Work?" roared Gabriel from the stage, "Health and Safety at Work? Non-existent, it would appear, as far as we angels are concerned. We were sent down, unarmed and unprepared, into hostile territory, into a potential war zone. And the outcome? One of our members, a young and innocent angel, has been spirited away, no doubt by the forces of evil. And what, you may ask, are the authorities doing about it?" He paused to sweep his challenging gaze over the sea of upturned faces. "Our so-called new leader, 'Saint' Hiram, has gone walkabout and his assistant is reported to be consulting the ouija board in desperation for the answer. I say that it's about time Heaven was reclaimed by the Holy. I propose that we go to the remaining Trustees and demand that something be done. Are you with me, Comrades?" The angels cheered in solidarity.

"And another thing," continued Gabriel, "we're not going to sit on our backsides while one of our little sisters is in danger. We'll be sending down a crack team of investigators from the G.A.'s office to search for her."

* * *

Jake looked round the cottage, furnished in prettily co-ordinated fabric, hearts and cherubs, pink and white frills, and cushions as squidgy as the marshmallows Tracey was so fond of. He felt as if he would drown in all the sweetness of it. Tracey, on the other hand, was enthralled. She darted from room to room, uttering cries of delighted admiration. She nearly swooned when she saw the shelves stocked full of romantic novels and films, the fridges crammed with enormous boxes of chocolates and bottles of pink champagne, and huge baskets of red roses in every corner of the cottage.

"How wonderful it will be, to be together, here," she said.

Jake shook his head slowly, a sad expression on his face. "That wouldn't be wise, Princess. For one thing, we don't want to ruin your reputation, and I need to spend some time with my colleagues." It wasn't far from the truth. Satan had put his hoof down. There was no way he'd trust Jake under the same roof as the angel for any length of time and Jake had to agree – he didn't trust himself either. With his thumb he wiped away a tear from Tracey's cheek. "We don't want them getting suspicious, do we? You leave it to me. Just stay here out of sight until I can think of some way for us to be together, forever. Besides, I want to be good enough to ask you to marry me." He kissed her, very quickly. "Don't worry, I'll come and see you as often as I can. In the meantime, enjoy yourself here, think of the things we can do once we are together. We could go to the Paris Opera House, float down the Grand Canal in Venice in a gondola, gaze at the starlit sky from the deck of a cruise liner, hold hands on a deserted, tropical beach, lean over a bridge and watch the river flow underneath. Don't you remember? Those were Laura's dreams, but they can be our future. Like I said, our story is going to have a happy ending." He lifted her hand and raised it to his lips. "Now, I must go. Be brave for me, for both of us."

* * *

* * *

Hiram had fled to Death Valley to think about what he had
discovered and to mourn his betrayal. It was a double betrayal, by
Pammy and by God, the two people whom Hiram had thought he
could trust. He wasn't sure which was worst; Pammy for arranging
his murder, or God for not telling him the truth, for letting him find
out like this. How Peter and the others must be laughing at him,
for surely they knew, had probably known all along. He sat brooding
for forty days, and then became aware that his surroundings had
changed. The colour of the sand was different and there were
unfamiliar coloured lights in the night sky. He was still in a desert,
but in a desert on a distant planet in the galaxy of Andromeda, and
beside him, still engrossed in His computer games, sat God.

"What did you expect me to do?" God said, without taking His
eyes away from the screen. "If I'd told you, you would never have
believed me. You had to find out for yourself."

"Sure I would have believed you. When have I ever not believed
in you?" said Hiram bitterly.

"Maybe," said God, "but you wouldn't have thanked me for it.
Besides, you were happy in your ignorance."

"You must have known that I would find out." Hiram paced up
and down, wearing a furrow in the purple sand.

"Not necessarily. It was your choice to go down to Earth. You

180

have free will, remember? What's done is done, we can't change it, we just have to decide how to deal with it."

"Deal with it? Whadaya expect me to do?" Hiram stopped pacing and turned to God, "I'm sure not going back, Second Coming or no Second Coming."

"Oh don't worry about that," said God. "What are you going to do about your wife?"

"Isn't that more in your line – divine retribution? 'Vengeance is mine' saith the Lord, isn't that how the story goes?"

"I wasn't thinking in terms of revenge. I've long since grown out of my vengeful, Old-Testament God phase. It served its purpose, in its time, but times have changed. I'm more of what you'd call a 'New God', a caring and sharing, compassionate, happy-to-help-round-the-house type of God. Ask yourself, Hiram, why she did it. Was it your fault? Did you ever ask her what she really wanted from life?"

"So you're telling me that I'm to blame for my own murder?"

"All I'm saying is that perhaps you should think about it. Did you ever consider her needs?"

"She wanted what I wanted, it was our dream, the both of us."

"Was it? Or did you just sweep her along in your current, drown her in your dreams?"

"So, whadaya saying? That I should have let her indulge herself by spending a fortune on clothes and jewellery, instead of carrying out your work?"

God turned and looked at Hiram for the first time. "So you think that's what she really wanted? You don't know her very well, do you, Hiram? More importantly, you never listened to her. She wanted nice things, that was true, but what she really wanted was babies. And you said it was the wrong time, that she had to wait until you'd achieved your dream. It was never the right time, was it, Hiram? And after a while, she gave up asking and you forgot all about it."

181

"I kinda thought she'd changed her mind. Anyway, there was still time."

"Time slips away too quickly. She heard her biological clock ticking, slower and slower, fainter and fainter. She knew that the battery was running low."

"She could have insisted, she could have left me. Oh God, she didn't have to kill me."

"You have a point. All I'm saying is that it wasn't just clear cut, black and white. To some extent, you were the engineer of your own downfall."

Hiram sat down on the sand, head in hands. "So you're telling me that I should forgive her? That'll take some time, some thought, that's if I ever can."

"It's not a question of forgiveness, Hiram. It's gone beyond that, now. The question is, are you going to save her? She's with the Devil now, you know."

"Then I guess she's lost for ever."

"Not necessarily. She's still on Earth, not yet in Hell. And, more importantly, she hasn't really gone of her own free will. Think about it, Hiram, but don't take too long. If you do want to try to save her, I'll help."

* * *

Edith cursed to herself as she made up yet another bed. Five extra guests in the big house and one in the cottage, and no extra staff. And she couldn't get Duncan to lift a finger to help, either. He was too busy, laughing and joking with Satan and his demons, drinking and playing cards until the small hours of the morning. Edith didn't like the way things were going. It was one thing being a would-be glamorous Satan worshipper, dancing naked round the fire, chanting and performing strange rituals, but this was another thing altogether. This was turning nasty.

It was seeing that woman which had first brought it home to Edith. Poor thing; she didn't know where she was or who she was, she just floated around, her feet two inches from the floor, her eyes large and glazed, her mouth open. She hadn't spoken a word, or moved of her own volition; she just sat down or stood up, moved or stood still, according to Satan's commands. The Devil had entertained Duncan and the demons with a display of how, with a click of his fingers, he could make the woman dance, like a puppet doll, until she was exhausted. Edith was sickened by the way the others, including Duncan, had laughed as they clapped and cheered. And she'd noticed how Mephistopheles, when Satan wasn't watching, would spitefully pinch the woman.

Then there was the other one, little more than a child – an angel, they'd bragged – whom they had installed in the cottage. Edith sometimes saw her, a pale face at the window, watching and waiting. The demon called Jake visited her every day, but he didn't stay long. Edith had heard him boast to the others about how easily he had tricked her, how he could get her to do anything for him. The others had laughed. Edith was discovering a lot of things. It was one advantage of being treated as if she were invisible. It had reached the stage where they didn't even look up when she walked into the room, let alone stop talking. They would just carry on talking over their loathsome plans, while she dusted the shelves or cleared away the tea things.

Until now, Edith had not fully appreciated the depth of evil that her faith represented. She had listened unquestioningly to Duncan's smooth arguments that Satan was not really the "baddie" of the story, that he was just another god, who'd had a raw deal from his rival. According to Duncan, Satan hadn't had the same opportunities as Jehovah; he was a victim of propaganda. If Satan had managed to get his book on the market before God had published his bestseller, The Bible, it would have been a different story altogether. In Duncan's version, God had been in the right place at the right

183

time, had blackened poor Satan's name and pushed him into a hole in the corner existence. But now, Edith could see the reality of a powerful being who treated women as mere objects, making helpless toys of Pamella, the angel and also Edith herself. Nowadays, even Duncan treated her as little more than a skivvy. However, she thought of poor, glamorous Pamella, and, if that was what a woman got for being attractive, Edith was starting to think that she was better off staying as she was: plain, dumpy, but comparatively safe.

The other thing worrying Edith was the money. She'd been horrified at the size of some of the bills coming in; for the hire of Wembley, publicity material, recording Satan's album and for computer equipment. Edith couldn't for the life of her imagine what the Devil wanted with computers. She'd taken Duncan to one side and asked him where all the money was coming from. Their funds were by no means inexhaustible; much of it was tied up in the bricks and mortar of the estate. Edith suspected that Duncan had mortgaged the place to the hilt. But when she'd expressed her concerns, he'd just sneered and told her, "What does it matter? It's just a drop in the ocean compared with what we'll have when it's all over." It was a side of Duncan she hadn't seen before and she didn't like it. This was not the old, amiable Duncan, a dabbler in the black arts, just looking for an extra edge of excitement to his life. Now, he was greedy, manipulative and cold. He paid her no attention, he was too busy drinking and plotting with his demon friends.

That was perhaps the worst revelation of all, the hardest for Edith to bear. After twenty-seven years of marriage, and raising two children, now grown-up, Edith felt as if thick scales had fallen from her eyes. All Duncan could think about was power, all he could talk about was how Satan was going to take over the world, with Duncan as his left-hand man. Edith was more pragmatic; somehow she couldn't see it working out quite that way. It was all very well while they had their uses, but as soon as the Devil had drained every last resource out of them, she didn't think they stood a cat in Hell's chance.

Edith didn't know what she could do about the situation, but she was sure about one thing; she wasn't going to sit back and let Duncan drag her down with him.

* * *

It was printed, in full colour, on the front page of every national tabloid newspaper, and on the inside pages of many of the broadsheets. It was the photo-journalism scoop of the year, perhaps the decade: the Ghost Coach, hurtling round the Big Dipper at Blackpool Pleasure Beach.

CHAPTER 13

As soon as Julia finished reading the message from God, she became aware that something was happening to her surroundings. The tables, the people, the whole room, seemed to be dissolving away. Disorientated, she took a step forward and realised that she was treading on a soft, shifting surface. She looked down. Sand. Purple sand. She looked up. A few yards away, there was a figure; someone sitting at what looked like a computer terminal. She approached the figure cautiously.

"Hello," said the figure. "I'm God. Please excuse me for not shaking hands, I'm a little busy at the moment."

"Hello," said Julia nervously, unsure how she was supposed to address God.

"Don't worry," He said, reading her mind. "I'm not one for protocol. Don't worry," He repeated to Himself, "I seem to be saying nothing else nowadays, I was only just saying to Hiram . . ."

"Hiram?" interrupted Julia, forgetting who she was talking to. "Has he been here, is he all right?"

"He'll be fine, he's had a bit of a shock, that's all." He turned to her and smiled. "Ah, good. Here are the others."

Julia looked round. Peter, Paul, Maggie, Gabriel and Raphael were walking towards them, all looking perplexed, some even annoyed.

"I hope this will save me some time," said God. "I want to say one thing to you, once and for all. DON'T WORRY. Everything is under control. I want you just to go back to Heaven, and go about

186

your daily lives. If I need you, any of you," He looked at each of them in turn, in a way that made it perfectly clear that He knew every thought, every intention, "I will get in touch."

"But, Lord," said Peter, "It's chaos in Heaven. No offence to this lady," he looked at Julia, "but she just doesn't have the experience."

"I suppose you think you can do better, do you, Peter? I suppose that's why you couldn't wait to hand the job over to a consultant? You leave Julia to carry on for the time being. She's doing a fine job under the circumstances. Now, go back. I've got a lot of work to do." He turned back to His computer and His visitors found themselves transported back to Heaven.

Paul spoke first. "Well, if that isn't the most . . ."

"Shut it," said Maggie, "you heard what He said. Let's just get on with it."

* * *

"I'm very pleased with the way things are going," said the Devil. He was relaxing with Duncan and the other demons while Edith was laying the table. They were listening to Satan's new album.

HELLTEL presents
SYMPATHY FOR THE DEVIL
15 Infernal Classics
featuring
Sympathy For The Devil – The Rolling Stones * Dance
With The Devil – Cozy Powell * That Ole Devil called
Love – Billie Holliday * Bat Out Of Hell – Meatloaf *
Rainbow Demon – Uriah Heep * Straight To Hell – The
Clash * The Devil's Answer – Atomic Rooster * Fire –
The Crazy World Of Arthur Brown * Hellraiser – The
Sweet * Disco Inferno – The Tramps * The Devil Came
Down To Georgia – The Charlie Daniels Band * Devil

Woman – Cliff Richard * Devil Gate Drive – Suzi Quatro
* Devil In Disguise – Elvis Presley *
Losing My Religion – REM

"Brilliant," Satan pronounced as the last track finished playing. "This blasts Heaven's pathetic effort right off the planet. And look at the Cliff Richard track, that's a bit of an own goal on the part of the God Squad. Now, Duncan, how is the Infernet coming along?"

"Very well," Duncan informed him. He had been puzzled when the Devil had ordered him to purchase expensive computer equipment, but as soon as he had explained his scheme, Duncan had marvelled at the idea. The Devil was setting up a network which linked Devil worshippers; home to home, nation to nation. Already, after only a couple of weeks, the Net had spread out from Britain to Europe, the Americas, Asia, Africa and the Antipodes. Already, thousands of devotees were linked up, sending messages of support and awaiting instructions.

"I think we're ready then," said the Devil, "to send out our first invitations." He sat down at the computer terminal and tapped out his message on the keyboard.

HIS SATANIC MAJESTY cordially invites his loyal
followers to ARMAGEDDON at WEMBLEY STADIUM on
25th December at Midnight RSVP

The message was transmitted to all subscribers to the Infernet by electronic mail. But there was one message that couldn't be sent that way, that had to be hand-delivered. So Damien was sent to drive through space in the black limousine to a large mansion, neither in Heaven nor in Hell.

Damien stepped out of the car, walked up to the front door, and popped an envelope through the letterbox.

Inside the house, a robed figure bent down to pick up the

envelope. "What's this then? It's not often we receive correspondence." He opened it and took out a fire-edged card. "Hurry," he called to his comrades. "Saddle up the horses, our services are required."

* * *

The authorities in Heaven were not the only ones who had been worried about Hiram's disappearance. Alexander X sat in the luxury of the Papal apartments, burning inside with cold anger. He was not a man who took kindly to being double-crossed, especially now that he was Pope. He'd been tempted by a golden business opportunity and, although he'd been sceptical at first, once he'd got a feel for the project, he was a man obsessed. He wasn't going to sit back now and let the chance of an eternity slip through his fingers.

There were traditional methods of dealing with this kind of situation. The trouble was that they would be ineffective on an already deceased person. But there was another way, there were living people, loved ones, of whom the American was reportedly extremely fond. Alexander's agents were at this very moment on their way to Georgia, where they would invite Hiram's widow to an exclusive audience with the Pope. It would be an invitation she could not refuse.

Alexander's thoughts had also turned to the Protestant contingent, to the beautiful lady archbishop and her minions. He had no doubt that those treacherous turncoats were behind the mystery. It was obvious that they had grasped an opportunity to negotiate an exclusive deal with the American. Alexander had no intention of letting the Godless bastards get away with it. He had an expert surveillance team keeping watch on the archbishop, scrutinising her every move.

Alexander's private 'phone rang. It was Carlo, with bad news.

189

The American broad had disappeared, together with her new husband, Hiram's business manager. Carlo said that the place was crawling with cops, who had been called in to investigate the disappearances and had found material that raised suspicions about Hiram's death. But Alexander was not one to give up; after all, he was Pope, and Popes were supposed to be infallible. Alexander had connections, a network of churches and believers that spread out to every nation on the Earth, and if those people were out there, he would find them.

* * *

In her gingerbread cottage, Tracey flitted round the room like a tiny white butterfly, drawing in the scent of the flowers through her delicate nostrils. Then she would sink back into the plump cushions, sipping the pink champagne, nibbling at the chocolates and gazing at the scenes being enacted on the television screen. The more films she watched, the more sweetness she tasted, and the more she became enmeshed in the sticky, deadly web of it all.

Every once in a while she would become distracted from whatever was happening on the television screen; moments when, surrounded by all the things she enjoyed, she couldn't understand why she felt so empty. Jake still came to see her, but usually no more than once a day. He said that to visit more often would put her in danger; he didn't want his colleagues to become suspicious. When he was there, he would say such lovely things to her, and would kiss her, briefly, chastely. She knew that there was more to love than that. Not, she thought shuddering, the frantic couplings which had been shown in some of the more contemporary films. Instead, she was thinking of the passionate kisses and embraces that even the dutiful Laura and Alec had shared in Brief Encounter. That was the kind of love she wanted, she knew it existed, for it was there, in those old films, in those paperback novels. It was the kind of love that manifested itself in yearning gazes and longing, lingering kisses, but which never moved beyond the bedroom door. She was thankful that Jake didn't seem to want that sort of thing. The other men did, in the films, in the books; they were all the same, manfully crushing the woman in their embrace, bruising their lips. Perhaps, she thought, he was too much of a gentleman.

The door of the cottage opened and Tracey ran, smiling, to greet her lover. But it was only the lady who came every couple of days to tidy up and make the bed. Tracey smiled, a sweet, disappointed smile, then went back to her films, a prisoner of love in her honey-trap.

* * *

Gloria had been annoyed when she was asked to help with the investigation on Earth. She had felt so near to making a breakthrough in her search for Martin and the other missing men, but then she couldn't really refuse to help a fellow angel, an angel in distress. Besides, if she did find the angel, it could give her career a much bigger boost than simply finding some insignificant human beings.

Gloria had thoroughly researched this case. She'd spoken to everybody who had known Tracey, and had learned all about her likes and dislikes. Finding her first real lead had been easy. She had called in at the Tourist Information Centre and told the assistant that she was in the City for a few days and wanted information about the best places to go. She loved romance, she had told the woman, books, films, that sort of thing, perhaps there was a museum? The woman had consulted a *What's On* magazine, then had directed Gloria to a small, back street cinema where a festival of romantic films was being shown.

She soon knew that she was on the right trail. At first, the cashier looked vaguely at Gloria when she described Tracey. The incident had happened a few weeks ago, and was soon forgotten, but something was pulling it gently to the front of her mind. "Yes, I remember, a young girl. Something about you reminds me of her." Gloria had come across this sort of thing before: "You all look the same," people would say, as if they couldn't see past the wings and the halo. In reality, Gloria was tall and dark, totally unlike the fluffy blonde Tracey. But Gloria smiled patiently at the woman, told her that they were sisters and asked her to remember as much as she could about the girl.

The woman paused. "She was with a young man, I'm sure. He was dark, rather good-looking in a roguish sort of way. There was something funny about them, I can't quite put my finger on it. They stayed here for two full days, sat through the films twice."

Elsie, the cashier from the sweet kiosk, joined them. "Wasn't that the time we had all that trouble, Cynthia?" she interrupted. "That stuff in the tills?"

"Oh, yes," Cynthia agreed. "And I remember you saying afterwards that you thought that young man had something to do with it."

"Well it did only happen on those two days when he was here and, anyway, I didn't like the look of him," Elsie shivered, "he looked a bad lot. But she was ever so sweet."

"Did you see where they went when they left?" asked Gloria.

"No, but we were talking to Jack, that's the usher, afterwards, and he was saying that they had gone off in ever such a hurry. He said it was strange, as if the girl hadn't realised how long they'd been there."

Gloria thanked them both. She could only guess that, if Tracey had realised suddenly that she'd been at the cinema for two days, her first instinct would have been to try to join the others. But if that was the case, and Tracey had gone straight back to the coach park, she would have found the others, who had waited three days. Gloria tried to put herself in Tracey's shoes, and thought what she would have done, lost and confused in a strange place.

Then she headed towards the railway station, the place where Tracey had been working before she went missing.

* * *

Edith briskly stripped the bed – just one more in a seemingly infinite queue of beds to be dealt with. She had recognised the look of disappointment on the little girl's face – she was pining for her worthless lover. Edith had heard enough snippets of conversation to realise who the girl was, and what the demons intended to do with her.

Edith had strict orders not to converse with Tracey. If the angel spoke to her, she was to say that she was only a cleaning woman who was too busy to talk. So far, she had obeyed this command, and had responded to the angel's friendly greeting with a curt nod and an abrupt "Good morning". It had suited Edith. Knowing what she knew, she could barely look the angel in the face, let alone speak to her. But the angel had continued to smile sweetly and greet her warmly. The more Edith saw of her, the more she thought how naive, how trusting she was, how ripe for betrayal. It made her very angry.

Edith thought of herself. She'd lived the best part of her life and had wasted it. She'd raised two children and where were they now? Selfish and greedy adults whom she rarely saw. She had nothing to show for her life, had added nothing to the world. And now, back there in the big house, real Evil lurked within her walls and plotted loathsome, diabolic deeds. If Edith let that happen without a word of dissent, she would be complicit in the evil, an accessory to the crime. Now was the time for Edith to make a difference, to do something that would really count. She tucked in her hospital corners and went downstairs to confront the angel.

Tracey was watching a film. She turned and smiled as Edith entered the room. Edith paused for a moment. She realised the danger of what she was going to do and knew that it was not too late to stop. She could just tidy up, take away the empty sweet wrappers and leave without a word. She looked down at the angel's large, blue eyes, upturned and almost pleading, and took a deep breath.

"You must leave, get away from here."

"What do you mean?" Tracey asked.

Edith sat on the edge of the settee. "You're in great danger. They mean to kill you, to sacrifice you, on Christmas Day."

Tracey's eyes widened. "Have Jake's friends found out about me?"

Edith laughed. "He's been in on the whole thing from the start. He was sent to lure you here."

"That's not true." Tracey stood up. "He loves me, he's going to marry me. If you'd heard the lovely things he says to me you wouldn't dare to tell these lies!"

"I know all about that." Edith stood up, too, and grasped Tracey's arm. "It's all make-believe. I heard him boasting to the others about it. He's been acting, just like in those romantic films that you're so fond of. He's been feeding you the same sort of lines that they used, to pretend that he's in love."

"No, no," screamed Tracey. "You're lying, you're jealous." She pulled her arm away from Edith's grip, covered her ears with her hands and screwed up her eyes.

"Don't be silly, everything loving he's ever said to you is a pale imitation of what the characters say in Brief Encounter, or in the other films you've watched together."

At the mention of that film, the one Jake had said was "their film", Tracey opened her eyes. How did this woman know about their special film?

"I'm not lying," insisted Edith gently, "I only want to help. They're evil, Satan and the demons, they're plotting something terrible. You've got to run away, get as far away from this place as you can."

"Satan? Here?"

"Yes, he's at the big house, with the others, with Jake."

Tracey shook her head, slowly. "I don't believe it."

"Think about it, but the longer you delay, the harder it will be for you to pull yourself away. I must go, they'll get suspicious. I've taken a terrible risk to come here and warn you, it's up to you now." She walked out of the room, leaving Tracey in a state of semi-shock.

Tracey collapsed into the cushions, thinking of Jake. The way he looked at her, the things he said. That woman must be mistaken, she didn't know Jake, not like Tracey did. But she remembered the woman saying that the sacrifice was going to take place at Christmas, which Tracey knew would coincide with Hiram's plans for the Second Coming. Then there was the film she'd known about, Brief Encounter. Tracey knew that there was only one way to find out for sure. She delved among the pile of video tapes, hesitantly picked out the film, loaded it into the machine, then gravely sat down to watch.

* * *

Gloria's hunch had been right, Tracey had returned to the station, with the strange young man after leaving the cinema. With a little gentle angelic coaxing the staff at the station had remembered her. The girl at the burger bar remembered them ordering cokes, then sitting huddled together, sadly and silently, as if it were the end of the world.

"Did you notice anything else happening on that day, anything unusual?" asked Gloria.

The girl remembered there being some trouble with the till. There had been horrible slimy stuff all over the money. They'd had the same trouble at the ticket office, and she'd heard talk of it

195

happening on one of the trains, in the buffet car.

Next, Gloria interviewed the ticket office clerks, and soon found the one who had issued two tickets for the young couple, tickets for the 22.15, the last train to Meddlesham. He confirmed the story about the slime in both his till, and the one on the train. "It was nasty, smelly stuff, ruined most of the bank notes and stripped all the print and writing from the cheques," he told her. "My boss was livid."

Gloria thanked him and walked away. She now knew for certain that Tracey was in the company of evil. She slipped unnoticed past the ticket inspector and sat down to wait for the next train to Meddlesham.

* * *

The Infernet spread its evil web around the world, the threads permeating to every corner where evil lurked. So it wasn't long before Alexander X came to hear about it. With his contacts, it was a simple matter to get linked up to the Infernet, and now he sat with his trusted henchmen, Carlo and Marco, reading the message on the screen.

"Very interesting," he remarked. "This might be worth a closer look, my friends. I want you to trace where these messages are coming from. I think I should meet this Satan; he sounds like a man I might be able to do business with. Maybe he can lead us to the American."

* * *

Tracey stumbled through the woods, her vision blurred by tears. She had watched the film with alerted eyes, and listened to the words with attentive ears; and as she had done so, parallel images had run through her head: Jake looking at her in the same way, saying the same sort of things. He hadn't even confined himself to the man's role, but had lifted sentiments and expressions from both Trevor Howard and Celia Johnson. He had been laughing at her all along, presenting her with a mockery of love and she'd fallen for it like a trusting fool.

She had been so stupid, so blind. The sense of humiliation stung her, particularly when she remembered Jake's aborted suicide attempt. She should have realised then that, as a spirit on Earth, he could not have been harmed. She would never be so innocent, so gullible, again. She was free of all that. She burst out from the trees and started to march determinedly down the country road towards the town that she could see in the distance.

* * *

Gloria stepped down from the train and again successfully dodged the ticket inspector. It was a small station, situated in the rural Midlands. Outside, Gloria consulted the map on the wall, then headed towards the centre of the small market town. She instinctively felt that she was close to achieving her goal. She hadn't yet reported back to her office, not wanting to be beaten to the post by one of her ambitious colleagues. There would be plenty of time for sharing the good news, when she had Tracey safely under her wing.

* * *

Up in Heaven, a new spirit of co-operation had emerged. Julia was chairing a case conference to discuss the disappearance of the Angel Tracey. Saints Peter, Paul and Mary Magdalene, and the Archangels Gabriel and Raphael were present, and for once they were all in agreement. It was getting close, dangerously close, to the big event, and the implications of having an angel at the mercy of the enemy were horrendous. Gabriel suspected that she would be used as a hostage or, possibly, as part of a Satanic ritual. The only thing to do was to make the angel mortal again. Julia nodded sadly. "It's what she's always wanted anyway, to be alive, down on Earth."

* * *

In the town of Meddlesham, the local residents had been actively and vociferously campaigning for years for the construction of a bypass. They were fed up with the heavy, dirty lorries which thundered through the High Street, shaking the quaint buildings down to their foundations, breaking the surface of the road, shattering their peace. In a few weeks from now, they would see the start of the work which would signal the end to their campaign; so just now they were content to look smugly on as the juggernauts roared through, for they knew their days were numbered.

Gloria emerged from the sub-post office, where her enquiries had drawn a blank. Suddenly, on the other side of the road, she noticed a small figure, dressed in white, walking towards her. Everything about her was lank and forlorn: her hair, her tattered dress, her drooping wings. Tracey's tear-stained eyes were cast down – she was obviously making sure to avoid the cracks on the pavement. Perhaps sensing the presence of another Heavenly being, she looked up, saw Gloria and smiled weakly. Gloria waved back. Tracey stepped out of the road, towards her.

Tracey did not see the coach that bore down on her. At the very instant she lost her wings, and was given the life that she so much yearned for, it was snatched straight back again.

Gloria, the coach driver, and fifty-two Japanese businessmen looked down in shock at the crumpled little body, lying in the road like a swatted butterfly.

CHAPTER 14

Julia blamed herself. If they'd only waited a little longer; if they'd only thought about it more carefully, Tracey would have survived the accident. Still, as Maggie had pointed out in her matter-of-fact way, there was no real harm done, Tracey was just back where she started. The fact that she'd absconded hadn't counted against her: it couldn't be a mortal sin, because Tracey hadn't been mortal at the time. And then, once she had become mortal, she hadn't lived long enough to sin. So she'd found herself, back in Heaven, with a shiny new pair of wings. But she wasn't the same Tracey. Somehow the light had gone out of her eyes. The archangels said that this was for the best. Once she'd settled down, she would be more content with her lot and therefore more efficient at her job. This experience, they said, would be the making of her. Having seen the angel's sad little face, Julia couldn't bring herself to agree.

As she pondered over the angel's fate, she found herself walking, without any real intent, towards the Paradise Cultural Complex and up the marble steps of the art gallery. She wandered through the rooms, taking no real notice of the pictures hanging on the wall, until she came to a room full of the work of the Impressionists. These had been particular favourites of Martin's, she remembered, then realised that this was the first time in what seemed like weeks that she'd thought of him.

She thought back to their honeymoon in Paris. Martin had said that it was his most favourite place in the world. He'd taken her to the Louvre, and shown her his favourite canvases, by Degas, Manet, Renoir and the others. It had been a wonderful holiday, marred only later by Martin's mother's spiteful revelation that he'd also taken Lucy there on honeymoon.

Julia walked slowly round the room, recognising some of the paintings. There was one at the end of the room that seemed to draw her attention. It was a small painting of a group of men sitting at a pavement cafe, sipping from tiny glasses and laughing. There, in the centre of the group, was the unmistakable figure of Martin.

Julia stopped, dead still. She looked again. Perhaps it was a trick of the light, enhanced by her memories. But she was sure that it was him. As she peered into the painting, she could swear that the figures moved, and talked and laughed. She could hear Martin's voice clearly, his faltering schoolboy French, his reserved laugh. She looked over to the brass plaque fixed to the side of the picture. Edouard Manet was the artist, the title, "Artist and Friends, Montmartre, 1926". She knew without having to consult a reference book that everyone in that picture had been dead by that date. So now she knew where Martin was. A sense of relief swept over her, and she felt only happiness for him. He was in a place where he wanted to be, where he would be happy, and she would keep his secret.

She took one last look at the picture, then turned and walked away. She knew, without looking back, that the picture would fade, that no-one else would ever see it and that Martin would be safe. The angelic tracker dog, Gloria, had lost interest now, fêted as a heroine after finding Tracey, even though she had lost her again so quickly. Gloria was now busy writing a series of articles about her experiences for *The Herald*. And as for Lucy, she had found herself a cause, fighting for the rights of first wives, but had seemed to have forgotten why she had set up the campaign in the first place. By keeping Martin's whereabouts a secret, Julia felt that she would always have a part of him in her heart.

* * *

After her conversation with Tracey, Edith spent the next few hours feeling as if she stood on the edge of a precipice. She had no way of knowing whether the angel was still in the cottage and, if she was, whether she would say anything to Jake about Edith's warning. On the other hand, if she'd taken her advice and escaped, Edith knew that suspicion was likely to fall on her. She waited, feeling every minute drag by.

At the end of a day that had been both physically and emotionally exhausting for her, Edith sat in the drawing room with the others, watching the late night local news. A young, unidentified girl had been knocked down and killed in a hit-and-run accident in Meddlesham High Street. It was a small town, and no-one had been reported missing, so the police had agreed to a photofit being shown on television, in the hope that someone knew where she'd come from. Edith watched, in horror, as an accurate likeness of Tracey's face appeared on the screen. Jake immediately jumped up and ran to the cottage.

Unheard, in the background, the news report continued . . .

"Police have not confirmed rumours that the coach reported to have been involved in this tragedy is the same coach that they have been seeking in connection with a recent M1 motorbike pile-up . . ."

As they waited for his return, Edith was sure that her face was burning, advertising her guilt, and that the Devil was studying her closely. She dared not look at him, just kept her eyes focused on the television screen. Moments later, Jake returned, breathless and agitated. "She's gone," was all he could say.

"You must have been careless, Jake," drawled Satan, relaxing back in his chair, "Perhaps you weren't as attentive as you might have been. This isn't going to do your reputation any good, is it?" He laughed lightly, too lightly.

"I thought she was convinced," said Jake, "she seemed to take it all in."

"Never mind," said Satan. "We have our insurance policy, and I'm sure that she is just as valuable as the angel. After all, while God's away, Hiram is the nearest best thing. He'll be devastated if anything nasty happens to his wife."

"After what she did to him?" said Mephistopheles.

"He'll forgive her. They always do, these Christians." He smiled at Jake, at Edith. "We're all tired. Let's go to bed. We'll plan tactics in the morning."

As Edith trudged slowly upstairs, she could hardly believe that the Devil had taken it so well. She felt sad for the angel, but was comforted by the belief that she'd escaped a far worse fate.

* * *

"What are we going to do about the Japanese?" asked Julia.
"At the moment, they're neither dead nor alive. We could take a lead from what happened to the angel – give them back life, then stage manage an immediate fatal accident," suggested Peter.

"That sounds terribly cold blooded," said Maggie.

"We can't just let them carry on roaming the Celestial highways, knocking people down left, right and centre," said Julia, rather angrily, as she thought of poor Tracey. "Somehow we have to get them back here, but under Heaven's control."

"Oh, please not," said Maggie. "Look at the havoc they wreaked last time. Valhalla is still out of bounds and there's nowhere else where you can really let your hair down."

"Let's make a Heaven specially for them," suggested Peter, "preferably a long way from the rest of us. We'll make it like Las

Vegas and Disneyland all rolled into one. That should keep them long enough for us to get them properly logged in to our systems."

"All right," agreed Julia, "we'll leave them where they are for the time being, and fetch them back when their new home is ready. If we can't think of another way, I suppose we'll have to do as Peter has suggested."

* * *

Edith hadn't slept well. She had been plagued by unsettling dreams and woken by strange aches and pains. She rose early as usual, ate breakfast, then waited for the others to get up so that she could start her chores.

"Don't rush off, Edith," said the Devil, as he took his seat at the table. "I've only just realised how much we've been taking your hospitality for granted. Here you are, rushing around, wearing yourself to a shadow, while the rest of us sit around, not lifting a finger to help." He smiled and patted the cushion on the chair next to him. "Come, sit here and relax. Duncan will do the bedrooms today, and Damien and Mephistopheles will cook. Today is going to be your day, Edith." He poured her a cup of coffee and offered her a cigarette, which she accepted with trembling hands.

Edith looked round the table at the demons, all smiling sweetly at her. Duncan was the only one not smiling, he just looked puzzled.

"Edith doesn't mind," he said, quickly. "She's used to it. She likes it."

"No, no." Satan shook his head. "I'm afraid that you're just as bad as the rest of us, Duncan. We haven't been paying nearly enough attention to Edith." He turned back to Edith and stood up; then, taking her by the hand, he led her to a full-length mirror which had materialised in the corner of the dining room.

"I know your dreams, Edith. I know what it is that you desire.

Today, you are to get your reward."

As Edith looked at her reflection in the mirror, the glass seemed to melt, distorting her shape like a trick mirror at a fairground. Then she realised that it wasn't the mirror that was moving, but her body, changing shape, lengthening and squeezing. She watched herself grow taller, slimmer, narrowing at the waist and filling out at the breasts and hips. Her grey, stubby, hair was oozing out from her follicles, becoming black and luxuriant. Her plump face tightened as her skin smoothed out over finely sculptured cheekbones, accentuated by large, almond eyes and Cupid's bow lips. Even her clothes were transforming, the faded tweeds darkening and growing sleek, sheathing her body in black satin. Eventually the image stopped moving, and Edith found herself gazing in wonder at the beautiful witch-woman in the mirror. Unsure whether it was an illusion, she looked down at her body, but it was all there, just as it was in the mirror.

"You can see, Edith," the Devil purred in her ear, "how I reward my loyal servants."

Edith lifted her long, slim hands with the scarlet-tipped fingers to her face and felt the smooth, soft skin. She ran her fingers through her thick, silky hair. It was all as real as it looked. A voice crept into her mind, "Mirror, mirror, on the wall, who is the fairest of them all?"

"It's wonderful, isn't it, Edith? It's what you've always wanted."

"Oh, yes," she murmured. Even her voice was different, low and husky. In the mirror she saw, behind her image, a reflection of the Devil, his smile widening, his lips drawing back over his fangs. Disquieted by his gaze, Edith looked quickly back at her own reflection.

A shiver ran through her body, followed by a tingling, burning sensation. As she stared at her reflection in the mirror, she saw the shapes change again, more slowly this time. She watched and screamed as the perfect breasts started to droop, the material of the dress stretched over a swelling stomach and pads of flesh grew round her hips, her arms, her thighs, under her chin, all accentuated by the taut, shiny material. She saw the lines appear at the corners of her eyes and mouth, her cheeks sagging until they were level with her chin. Opening her mouth in shock gave her a clear view of her teeth, yellowing, rotting, then dropping from the gums one by one.

Then all at once, everything seemed to shrink, to shrivel, as the dress no longer strained to contain the contents, but flapped loosely around her scrawny, bent body. With a final moan of horror, she watched the image blur as her old eyes clouded over and she felt, rather than saw, her whole fabric collapse into a lifeless pile of bones.

The mirror cracked from side to side.

Duncan watched the pile collapse into a small heap of dust which, caught by a slight draught from under the door, blew across the carpet into nothingness. He turned his widened eyes towards Satan. "Why?" was all he could say.

"There's no room for sentiment. She betrayed us, now she's got what she deserves." The Devil turned back to the breakfast table and started to tuck in to his bacon and eggs. "We'll have to make some changes round here, though. You'll have to pull your finger out, Duncan my boy. I'll say this for Edith, she was a good workhorse, you'll have a hard job living up to her standards. Best get an early start. The beds want making and you'd better vacuum this carpet." He turned to his demons. "I think we'd better install some security here, we don't know how much that angel knew about our plans. She's probably up there in Heaven right now, singing like a canary." He looked at Jake, who sat toying miserably with his food. "What's with the long face?"

"He's love-sick," sneered Mephistopheles. "Pining for his angel."

"Shut the fuck up." Jake bared his fangs. "Sorry, boss." He smiled at the Devil. "I was just thinking of the opportunity I've missed. If

I'd known that the silly bitch was going to throw herself under a bus, I might as well have screwed her and had done with it." He looked down at his plate and made a great display of scooping up a forkful of sausage, then looked at Satan again with a leer. "That would have been something to tell the lads back home."

"That's my boy," said Satan, slapping him on the back. Jake, his mouth full of sausage, spluttered and nearly choked. He kept a smile on his face, masking a feeling unfamiliar to him, a sense of loss and emptiness that he couldn't understand. His courtship, the word itself was alien to his nature, certainly hadn't gone the way he would have wished. His reluctant celibacy had meant that the time spent with the angel had been filled with conversation, usually him talking about himself and her listening in undisguised adoration. Now, when he thought of her, he remembered not the luscious, young, yet frustratingly forbidden curves of her body, but the way she had clung physically and emotionally to him. He couldn't understand this strange sense of loss. Jake had, for probably the first time in many existences, been someone's hero, the centre of another being's life. He had been needed, wanted, and, although he shuddered at the very thought of the word, loved. He'd had power over someone and that power had given him a new definition. But now it was all over and he was nobody again, just another demon in a horde of evil spirits, self-sufficient, self-contained and selfish, needing no-one, needed by no-one. He was jolted from his reverie by the sound of Satan's voice. Jake knew he mustn't let the others suspect that there was anything wrong.

"It's nearly time to bring the others here," the Devil was saying. "Our first full rehearsal at Wembley is only a week away. Perhaps a break would do you good, Jake. I know what a strain it must have been for you, having to keep your lecherous hands off the angel. So you can go back to Hell, round up the crew. Meanwhile," he looked at Mephistopheles and Damien, "I think we'll have to give Duncan a hand to get this place ready. Now that Edith has deserted us, it's all hands on deck."

* * *

Julia watched as the envelope floated down onto Hiram's desk. She could see smoke escaping from inside. Before she had time to pick it up, it was whisked away by an unseen hand.

In the desert of a planet in the galaxy Andromeda, God opened the envelope and took out the card. It was an invitation from the Devil, to Armageddon, and, at the bottom, a few words had been appended in Satanic scrawl: "Featuring human sacrifice, see enclosed photograph."

God fished the photo out of the envelope; it was Pammy, draped provocatively across a bed, her expression vacant.

"I think it's time for Hiram to make his decision," said God, to no-one in particular.

* * *

With Alexander's contacts, it hadn't taken long to trace the centre of the Infernet to Meddlesham Hall and to despatch his henchmen there to find out what was going on. Carlo and Marco, laden with sophisticated surveillance equipment, crept through Meddlesham woods in the moonlight. The inner edge of the wood marked the boundary of the estate, and the two men found themselves unable to penetrate any further.

"It's like some kind of force field," said Carlo, as he tried to push through the invisible barrier.

"Wow," said Marco. "This is powerful stuff, the boss is going to want to know how they do this. Let's try the equipment, we should be near enough to see something of what's happening."

From their rucksacks, they pulled out various gadgets: telescopes with high-powered lenses, night-vision glasses, sophisticated sound-magnification equipment. They set it all up, then looked, and listened. There was nothing. All they could see through the lenses was fog, and all the audio equipment picked up was a few crackles and hisses.

"We're wasting our time here." Carlo shook his head. "We'd better report back to the boss, ask what he wants us to do. We're dealing with big league stuff here, bigger than we could ever imagine."

* * *

Duncan wiped the sweat from his forehead. He wasn't used to this. Helping with the washing-up occasionally, or a little light dusting, that had been his limit in the past. Edith had done everything. He stopped work and sat on the bed, thinking of Edith, solid, dependable Edith, who had made sure that everything ran smoothly. Comfortable, undemanding Edith, she had cushioned him from the harsher side of life. Stupid, selfish Edith, she had deserted him, leaving him to cope on his own with only the half-hearted help of incompetent demons. Duncan wept with the bitter tears of a victim, cursing the woman who had betrayed him, the woman who had left him with all these beds to make.

* * *

The convoy of coaches, led by "EVIL 1", threaded its way through the country lanes, forcing other vehicles off the road, including a black van containing two dark-suited men and a plethora of sophisticated surveillance equipment.

Carlo and Marco watched through their shades. "Do you see what I see?" said Marco.

"It cannot be," said Carlo. Coachloads of horned demons sped past, faces pressed to the windows, forked tongues sticking out, and making obscene gestures. "The Holy Father will never believe this."

The coaches continued their journey to Meddlesham Hall, where they spewed out their diabolical passengers. After an undignified scrabble for cases and costumes, the demons burst into the Hall, and slid along the polished floors, whooping and squealing past a terrified Duncan before coming to an abrupt and subdued halt in front of the Devil.

"Let's have a bit of order," Satan's voice boomed forth, his arms folded across his chest. "You're not in Hell now, you know." He waited for the last of them to join the others. "You'll be shown to your rooms," he continued, "where you will unpack. We will assemble in the Great Hall," he pointed towards a door at the end of the entrance hall, "in exactly fifteen minutes time."

They swarmed up the sweeping staircase, the singers, dancers, conductor, orchestra, choreographer, composer, arranger, wardrobe mistress, make-up artists, hairdressers, scene painters, scene shifters, shape shifters, lighting technicians, special effects wizards, sound engineers, video engineers, stage hands, roadies, front-of-house staff, merchandisers, caterers and programme sellers. Some chattered and bitched, called each other "luvvie" or "darling" and clutched cases, hatboxes and make-up cases. Others lugged heavy boxes of equipment, called each other "mate" and made arrangements for wild parties after the show.

Duncan watched, stoically, as the stiletto heels scraped deep channels in the polished floor, as the cases gouged chunks of plaster from the walls, as the demons' sulphurous breath condensed on the soft furnishings, starting a slow, burning rot. It would all be over soon, he reassured himself.

* * *

The black stallions thundered at great speed through the cosmos, whipped almost to frenzy by their riders, the Four Horsemen of The Apocalypse, known affectionately as Sword, Famine, Plague and Wild Animals.

A voice boomed from behind, "Hold your horses, where do you lot think you're going?"

The noble steeds screeched to a halt. Famine turned round and fixed his hollow, hungry eyes on the speaker. His mouth gaped open. Plague turned, clutching his cowl around his scab-ravaged face. Wild Animals snarled and bared his teeth as he whipped round to challenge the speaker, then whimpered like a puppy when he saw the owner of the voice. Sword had unsheathed his weapon and brandished it high as he turned, ready for action.

"Oh, God, it's you," they cried in unison.

"I know perfectly well who I am," said God. "Now tell me what the Hell you think you're doing."

They looked at each other, the four fearless horsemen. Sword replaced his weapon, Famine and Wild Animals closed their mouths and Plague just looked sheepish, probably because he was carrying a particularly virulent strain of anthrax at the time.

Then Sword spoke. "It's time, isn't it? We got your message."

"I sent no message. Show it to me," demanded God.

Sword rummaged in his saddlebag. "It was here somewhere," he said, lifting out his sandwiches so that he could have a closer look. "That's funny, I'm sure I put it in here." He lifted out the scraps of blackened card, which were all that remained of the Devil's invitation, then inspected his sandwich for possible damage. "It's a good job that I like toasted cheese," he added, mournfully.

"Never mind about that," said God impatiently. "I know who sent that message and so do you. In fact, you should have known better all along. Haven't I always appeared in person when I've required your services?"

"Yes," admitted Sword, "we did wonder about that. But we knew you were busy and were not to be disturbed."

God sighed. "Just get back to your stables. I don't think I'll be needing you for some time." Hearing the sound of hoofbeats behind Him, He turned. "What's this?" He said as two more riders joined them.

"They're our new horsemen, or should I say horsepersons, equal opportunities and all that," said Sword, "I'm afraid they're a bit slow, they haven't been with us long."

God looked at the two approaching figures. The first was male, with a red nose bulging in the centre of a pale face. With four cigarettes in his mouth at once, he coughed and spluttered as, at the same time, he washed down brightly coloured pills with amber-coloured liquid, and tried to manoeuvre a hand-held computer game. As he moved, his bulging saddlebags clinked. The second was female, a glamorous brunette in a power suit, who was simultaneously operating a lap-top computer while juggling three mobile 'phones and a polystyrene cup full of black coffee. Instead of saddlebags, four briefcases hung from her saddle.

"May I introduce Addiction and Executive Stress," said Sword, "our new colleagues." He drew God to one side. "It's been a bit difficult for us lately, God. We just couldn't cope with the increased workload. As you'll appreciate, Plague, Famine and myself have been extremely busy, working flat out, for years. But frankly," he glanced briefly at the others, "Wild Animals hasn't been pulling his weight. It's not his fault, he's just become almost obsolete. It's this sophisticated weaponry that humans have developed. It's all he can do to manage the odd shark or crocodile attack these days." He shook his head and sighed. "But then we got to hear about these two. They were working freelance, so we kept an eye on them for a while. We were pretty impressed. Addiction's been operating for a good many years, Executive Stress is a relative newcomer, but they've both been reaping in significant numbers of casualties." He looked apologetic. "I know we should've asked you first, but with you being so busy . . ."

"All right," said God, "just don't let them get out of control. You know the bargain, you're entitled to no more than a quarter of the Earth. Don't exceed that limit, not until you're sent for, by me, and only me."

He watched as the Six Horsepersons of the Apocalypse turned and headed back to their base. A solar wind carried back a whisper of their conversation.

"Knock, knock."

"Who's there?"

"Armageddon."

"Armageddon who?"

"Armageddon out of this place."

CHAPTER 15

From the darkest corners, the dankest crevices, the blackest abysses, of the Earth, they emerged and started to converge on Wembley Stadium. They came by plane, by boat, by car, on foot. A black limousine with false number plates and darkened windows left Vatican City and headed for a small airfield where a private jet waited to take the occupants to another small airfield.

At nine-thirty on Christmas night, the gates of Wembley Stadium opened to swallow up Satan's faithful followers, who poured in to take their seats. Officially, there was no charge for entrance, but outside the Stadium, touts were offering tickets for the best seats. Three dark-suited men, wearing shades, secured for themselves, by means of a wad of crisp new banknotes, seats in the front row. Inside Wembley, official programmes, posters, compact discs, badges and T-shirts were being handed out by sultry demonesses dressed in tight black leather and fish-net tights. The T-shirts carried such messages as "ARMAGEDDON – BEEN THERE, SEEN IT, DONE IT, GOT THE T-SHIRT" and "MY DAD WENT TO ARMAGEDDON AND ALL HE BOUGHT ME WAS THIS STUPID T-SHIRT". The posters carried portraits of Satan, strutting in black leather. Outside, counterfeit merchandise was being exchanged for inflated prices. Narcotics were distributed freely.

A coach pulled up outside the stadium. The driver had despaired of finding anywhere different to take his passengers on Christmas night; he had presumed that there would be no entertainment available. This should be the answer to his prayers, a new experience for their increasingly jaded appetites. Fifty-two excited Japanese businessmen tumbled off the coach to join the queue for their first rock concert.

As the seats steadily filled up, the throbbing beat from Satan's compact disc pulsated out from giant speakers. From the wings, Satan looked on in satisfaction as demons warmed up the crowd by leading them in a series of Mexican waves. He'd just heard news from Jake, who had been sent to check out Earls Court. Satan had been delighted to hear that there was no sign of activity there. He smiled to himself. So God wasn't going to show, wasn't even going to put up a fight. It was as he had suspected, God was finished, burnt-out, dried up, weary of the world and ready for someone else to take over. Not that He would have had a choice. Satan grinned as he thought of Hiram telling the Heads of the Churches of his grandiose schemes. After today's no-show, God would lose any credibility He had left, and here was Satan, waiting in the wings to collect the bouquets. And he had recognised the dark-suited figure sitting in the front row. At last, he thought, an audience with the Pope.

The seats were all full now, those round the stadium and the extra seats which covered the pitch. There were even people sitting in the aisles and crammed in to every spare inch of space inside the perimeter. Satan watched their eager faces; he could smell their expectation. He signalled to the lighting engineers. The lights, which had been trained on the crowd, dimmed and a cheer went up from the audience. The lights now focused on the stage and, to the accompaniment of the throbbing beat of voodoo drums, the leather-clad Devilettes appeared, apparently from nowhere, to start their seductive bump-and-grind amid clouds of dry ice and jets of flame. The Devil strode onto the stage, modestly clad in a leather cat-suit and cape, and launched into the first number, his signature theme, "Sympathy for the Devil".

From out of the crowd came a voice of dissent from a leather-clad rock fan who had stumbled upon the gig by accident. "Not a patch on Guns'n'Roses," he remarked to his neighbour. From the stage, the Devil turned his gaze upon the speaker and, without faltering in his delivery, reduced him to a pile of smouldering ashes.

* * *

It was like looking down into a goldfish bowl, filled with little black ants instead of water, thought Hiram. God sat beside him on the cloud, cross-legged, occasionally chuckling at Satan's on-stage antics and giving a running commentary, for He could see in far greater detail than Hiram.

"I don't believe it, he's stripping off!" He squealed. "Yes, there he is now, strutting his stuff in a leather studded jockstrap."

Hiram strained to see, but it still looked like a goldfish bowl full of black ants.

"Oh." God frowned suddenly.

"What's the matter?"

"Nothing. He's left the stage."

"Is it over, then? What about Pammy?"

"It's not over. Can you hear the crowd? They're clapping, stamping their feet, calling for an encore."

Down on the stage, there was more dry ice, more jets of flame, more dancing Devilettes. At the rear of the stage, a platform rose and on it lay a woman, dressed in white.

"What's happening?" Hiram asked.

"He's building up to the climax," said God. He looked at His watch, it was five minutes before midnight.

"She's there, isn't she?" Hiram's voice was hushed. He couldn't make out what was happening on stage, but he had sensed the change in atmosphere, the build-up of tension.

"Yes," said God. "But don't worry, she's safe yet, Now, keep quiet, while I concentrate."

While Hiram strained his eyes to focus on flashes of light coming from the direction of the stage, God watched Satan sweep out in his full regalia of cape, horns and tail.

"What's he singing now?" whispered Hiram.

"I don't know the song," lied God. It was Elton John's "Sacrifice". He winced as the Devil drew a long curved blade from somewhere within the lining of his cape, and moved to the back of the raised altar.

Hiram noticed pinpricks of light dotted amongst the black of the crowd. "What's happening now?" he asked.

"They're lighting their cigarette lighters and swaying to the music," said God casually, hoping that Hiram couldn't make out the words the audience were singing along to the chorus, "It's a sacrifice, just a ritual death . . ." He looked down at Pammy, her eyes open but unseeing, and willed her to wake.

Lying prone on the altar, Pammy gradually became aware of a dark figure, standing over her.

The Devil gazed at her sadly. To have sacrificed an angel would have been a symbolic triumph of Evil over Good, which would have given him great powers. There was nothing special about this woman, she wasn't even a virgin, but it was still a human sacrifice, which would feed the bloodlust of the crowd, and it would bug the Hell out of Hiram.

Standing in the wings was Duncan, preparing to look away at the last moment. He had no appetite for real violence and was just thankful that the whole sordid mess would soon be over. The last week had been a nightmare, his house littered with feuding demon entertainers, the bathrooms cluttered with dripping tights and stage make-up. He had exhausted himself trying to clean up after them. He'd been too tired even to take advantage of Satan's generous offer of the pick of the female demons for a bedmate.

Jake stood beside Duncan. He had no qualms about the sacrifice, but felt a strange sense of relief that it was not Tracey lying on that altar.

Only Pammy, looking up past Satan into the dark sky, saw the certainty of impending death. A weak scream escaped from her parched throat, but she found herself unable to move. The Devil smiled. There was nothing he liked more than to see fear in his victims. But Pammy was not looking at him. Her eyes widened as she watched the black shape grow larger, blotting out the stars in an ever increasing circle.

"Repent, woman," hissed God through clenched teeth as the meteorite hung, momentarily suspended, above the stadium.

The Devil raised his blade. God raised His arm.

"Oh my God!" screamed Pammy.

"That'll do," said God, and released the Heavenly body to continue on its downward journey.

* * *

Moments later Hiram stared down at the smoking crater, which was all that was left of Wembley Stadium. "But you said you were gonna save her."

"I meant her soul, not her life."

Hiram shook his head at the scene of destruction. "That wasn't a very nice thing to do," he said, quietly.

"Perhaps not, but immensely satisfying. You've just seen vengeful Old Testament God in action, Hiram. Just be thankful that it doesn't happen very often."

"But to kill all those people." Hiram's voice was shaking.

God shrugged. "It was necessary. It'll give the human race a chance to get their act together."

"Have you destroyed Satan?"

"Of course not. A spirit cannot be destroyed. But he'll be a bit bruised and battered for a while – I've just destroyed a significant part of his power base."

"Only part?" asked Hiram, looking down at the crater.

"Hiram, surely you're not naive enough to think that all the evil on Earth could be contained by Wembley Stadium? All I've done is to wipe out some of the most powerful, organised Devil-worshippers. There's still plenty of evil left in the world, but this will be a savage blow to them. It should take them some considerable time to regroup their forces."

"And what about the Second Coming?"

"I hadn't forgotten. Wait here for a few minutes." God jumped off the cloud and drifted gently towards the Earth, His spirit diffusing as He neared the surface. He entered every household on the Earth simultaneously, speaking to every living person, either face to face or through their dreams. To each, He appeared in the form of the God they wanted to see, and His message was different and personal. With some people He left a gift – a talent or an idea; from others, He took away pain, disease or a bad memory. Afterwards, He erased all conscious memory of His visitation; but for the rest of their lives, people would remember that, for some elusive reason, that Christmas had been special.

God the spirit left the Earth and returned to Hiram, who sat, still slightly stunned, waiting on the cloud. "Let's go back to Heaven," He said, "we have things to straighten out."

* * *

In the kitchen of a large mansion, neither in Heaven nor in Hell, Sword and Plague sifted through a pile of application forms.

"What about this one?" Sword held up a blood-stained form. "Bloke who calls himself 'Horseless Carriages', specialises in motor vehicle accidents, plane crashes, sinking ships, punctured hot air balloons. His curriculum vitae is pretty impressive. What do you think?"

"Horseless Carriages?" Plague thought of his faithful steed, Spotted Dick. "No, I don't like the sound of it."

"He's been doing very well on a freelance basis," said Sword.

"Almost too well," said Plague, "going by these figures. He could make the rest of us redundant."

"All right," said Sword, "I get the message. We'll send the standard letter, 'Unfortunately we have no vacancies at present but we wish you every success in your future career.'"

"I'd prefer it," said Plague, "if you'd leave out the last bit."

"Just as you like. Now, who do we have here? 'Eating Disorders'. No, Famine would never stand for that, too much duplication."

* * *

Four battered and bedraggled figures limped into Hell, their tails between their legs, struggling through hordes of irate Satanists who were clamouring for vengeance against those who had lured them to their premature deaths. Satan and his henchmen were too exhausted to stay for Beelzebub's travesty of a welcome speech, delivered in monotonous tones from a face with a deadpan expression and accompanied by wooden gestures. They slipped, unseen, into Satan's apartments, to begin a long spell of convalescence. In the midst of the crowd, a deserted Duncan Crucible cursed the day when he'd first set eyes on his master.

* * *

On Earth, two stories dominated the pages of the world's press: the Wembley disaster and the mysterious disappearance of the Pope. Headlines screamed, "ROCK HORROR SHOW – FREAK METEORITE FLATTENS FANS" and "VANISHING VICAR OF ROME – MAFIA CONNECTION SUSPECTED".

In Heaven, the authorities were busy coping with the aftermath of the disaster, including the early and somewhat unexpected return of the Japanese businessmen, and a rather irate Italian gentleman who insisted that he'd been granted an unconditional place in Heaven and was resisting attempts to send him to the other place, where he was eagerly awaited by demons with freshly-sharpened pitchforks.

In a newly-constructed hotel on the outskirts of Heaven, Edith Crucible began her working day, starting on the first of over fifty beds that she would have to make in preparation for the arrival of a party of Japanese businessmen as permanent guests. She was resigned to her fate. Had it not been for her last act of kindness to the angel, she would now be in a far worse place. And there was hope; at the end of an appropriate period of community service, she would be free.

* * *

Thousands, no, millions of people must have passed him, the vagrant who stood motionless outside the entrance to Eternity Hall, his eyes staring blankly at the ground. He had been there for an immeasurable time when Martha found him.

"Poor thing," said Martha to Maggie, and laid her hand gently on his arm. He did not respond. "Someone's been looking after him. Look, he's had a haircut recently."

"Leave him be, Martha," said Maggie, a chill in her voice. "Don't you recognise him?"

"Yes, I know who he is, but I can't leave him like this. There is always a time for forgiveness."

"Not for him and, besides, he's not your responsibility."

"Of course he is," said Martha, her tone uncharacteristically abrupt, "I am in charge of Social Services." She gently led Judas away towards the New Limbo Hostel for the Temporarily Displaced. "Poor soul," she muttered, "his mind's gone."

She was right; his mind had gone, but it hadn't gone very far. Loosened from its moorings by Satan's sudden penetration and violent withdrawal, it had jumped out for a while, in search of the intelligence which had briefly inhabited it. Almost immediately, it had realised its mistake. It couldn't see, hear, or feel. All it could do was to think its way around. In a panic, it had sought out its original home, Judas's spirit form. After a time, what seemed like a very long time, it had felt a force attracting it towards its destination. It had sensed a warmth which told him that it was near, very near. Then, suddenly, the world had turned cold and the link had snapped.

Martha led Judas away, unable to see the invisible mind that squatted on the ground a few feet away.

"Oh, fuck," thought Judas's mind.

* * *

"I don't intend to abandon all of your new ideas," said God, as He helped Hiram clear out his office. "Take community service, for example. I wish I'd thought of it; much more constructive than Purgatory." He paused and looked thoughtfully at Hiram. "Have you seen her yet."

Hiram thought of Pammy, just starting her sentence of community service as a waitress in Valhalla. "No, I don't feel ready yet."

"The longer you leave it, the harder it'll be," advised God. "But it's your choice. You don't ever have to see her again if you don't want to."

"I'll probably come to terms with it, eventually," sighed Hiram.

"While we're on the subject of forgiveness," said God, as they packed up the last box and turned out the light, "I want to talk to you about Abe Dietrichson."

"Oh, no, absolutely no way."

"But perhaps an extra long period of community service, doing something unpleasant?"

"How unpleasant?"

"Mucking out the cages at Saint Francis' Zoo? Cleaning the toilets in Valhalla? Or even minuting the meetings of the Celestial Association of Minor Prophets?" He shuddered at the thought.

"I'll think about it," said Hiram, through clenched teeth.

"Good man." God slapped him on the back. "That's the spirit."

* * *

In the bar of the Wing and a Prayer, God expounded His philosophy of life to Hiram over a pint of Old Celestial. "The trouble with humans," He said, "is that they don't know how to relax. Up here, they have everything they could possibly want. They should be bursting into Heaven, full of energy and curiosity, looking for the answers to the questions they've always wanted to ask. I thought that they would search out their heroes, do all the things they've always wanted to do, stretch the boundaries, explore the possibilities." He took a mouthful of beer. "Instead, they come up here and settle down surrounded by mementoes of their Earthly life. I know that there are exceptions, Hiram, but on the whole, people just live extended versions of their past lives. I want them to exist on a higher plane, take advantage of all the opportunities. I give them freedom and they try to impose restrictions." He paused, draining the rest of His pint. "Ready for another?" Hiram nodded, and God passed His hand over the empty glasses, filling them again. "Things will have to change up here, Hiram, and I will start the ball rolling. From now on, I will be a new kind of God, a long-haired, sandal-wearing, hippie kind of God."

"Can I ask you something?" said Hiram.

"Go ahead."

"Was this planned all along?"

God took another drink before replying. "Of course. I knew that the Devil would never chance his hand unless he was convinced

222

that I had lost my grip."

"Supposing it had gone wrong?"

"Impossible." God shook His head. "I'm God, I'm omniwotsit."

"Omniwotsit?"

"Yes, any omni you can think of. Omnipotent, omniscient, omnipresent, omni . . ."

" . . . bus?" chipped in Hiram, nodding towards the party of Japanese businessmen who had stopped by for a few pints.

They both collapsed in helpless laughter. God was in His Heaven and all was right with the world.